W9-CHF-433

ARE
ALL · THE
GIANTS
DEAD · ?

by the same author

BED-KNOB AND BROOMSTICK

THE BORROWERS

THE BORROWERS AFIELD

THE BORROWERS AFLOAT

THE BORROWERS ALOFT

POOR STAINLESS

MARY·NORTON

Illustrated by Brian Froud

Harcourt Brace Jovanovich, Publishers
San Diego New York London

Originally published in Great Britain by J. M. Dent & Sons Ltd.

Library of Congress Cataloging in Publication Data

Norton, Mary.
Are all the giants dead?

SUMMARY: Finding himself in a land peopled with fairy-
tale characters, James attempts to help Princess Dulcibel
who is destined to marry a toad after her ball falls in the well.
[1. Fairy tales. 2. Fantasy] I. Froud, Brian.
[PZ8.N82Ar 1978] [Fic] 78-6622
ISBN 0-15-607888-0

Printed in the United States of America

B C D E F G H I J

To Oliver Knox
whose fault it was

Are all the giants dead?
And all the witches fled?
Am I quite safe in bed?

Giants and witches all are fled.
My child, thou art quite safe in bed.
—old poem

ARE
ALL · THE
GIANTS
DEAD · ?

ONE

When he awoke, the room looked different somehow: there was a window where the door used to be. No (how silly could he be?), the door was there on the other side of the wardrobe. And there had always been two windows. Hadn't there? Yes, of course, always two windows. And that soft, gray, thrumming light—vibrating light—neither dawn nor darkness. Every object looked still and clear: the electric fire, darkened now, stood outlined against the empty fire grate. And there was his picture of the running horse. Except now (he stared harder) the horse stood still with its head turned as though to look at him. Ah, this was the sign—or one of the signs: she must be here again, that lady.

He sat up in bed.

Yes, there she was, a little silvery, by the window writing in her notebook. Writing. Writing. He could see the pale bun of her hair. Beside her on the windowsill he seemed to see a scattered pile of papers—magazines, they looked like in the gradually strengthening light. Every now and again, she seemed to refer to them—lifting one from here and one from there and setting others aside. Soon she would look up. She did.

"Hello, Mildred," he said, smiling.

She laughed—that funny, half-shy, helpless little laugh. She always did this when he called her Mildred. He knew he should call her Aunt Mildred or Mrs. Somebody, or something like that. Her little laugh meant "What are children coming to?" and then that helpless, lingering smile meant "Never mind." But everybody else called her Mildred ("Dear Mildred, how nice to see you!" "How well you look, dear Mildred, not a day older!" "Who would remember us nowadays, dear Mildred, if you did not come?"). It wasn't his fault: he had never heard her other name.

"Hello, James," she said.

He began to get out of bed. "Where are we going?" he asked, as he disentangled his leg from his old leg. He no longer noticed the strange feeling this gave him—he was used now to walking about the room and still seeing himself lying there on the bed—a good imitation of himself, really, he thought, as he tightened up the cord of his dark red pajamas—a fair boy, straight, longish hair thrown out across the pillow, one arm flung wide. Even my mother, he thought, would take that for me. Mildred was very clever, sometimes, in the way she arranged things. Sometimes. Not always.

She was talking away now—in that excited, breathless little voice of hers. "And then . . ." she was saying, "we must go on to see Boofy and Beau. They are all great friends. . . ."

"All right," he said and watched her speculatively as she gathered up her books and papers, packing them neatly in her hand-embroidered Mexican satchel. He felt game for anything. Who were Boofy and Beau? he wondered. And who were those first people she had mentioned?

"Anyone dangerous?" he asked casually.

Mildred, standing up now, looked at him thoughtfully, her head on one side, as she adjusted a small pearl earring.

"You mean tonight?"

"Yes," he said, "after Boofy and Beau?"

"Well," said Mildred, glancing quickly at her notebook before snapping the elastic band around the covers and placing it in her satchel, "it depends on time." She felt in the pocket of her loose summer coat and drew out a pair of gray suede gloves—very new, they looked, and rather expensive. As she pulled them on carefully, stroking back the fingers, she glanced about the room. "Now, have we thought of everything?" (Very elegant, she looked, in that strange half-light. On the thin side, perhaps, and not what James would call young, but very elegant indeed.) "What sort of shoes are you wearing?"

"My moccasins," said James.

"Good. And better put on your leather jacket."

He followed her out of the room and weightlessly down the stairs. He always liked this feeling, a delicate push with one foot on the tread and a light, bouncing rise like flying. As usual, the stairs looked different; there was an unlikely bend to them. And the hall below looked quite unfamiliar, except for the grandfather clock and the two stuffed owls. It looked longer, somehow, and there were odd bits of furniture about. It occurred to him that Mildred had made it up from memory. The sticks in the umbrella stand were not at all like the ones he knew: they had never had a shooting stick, as far as he could remember—she must have just invented it.

Mildred, rather hastily and with a bit of secretive fumbling, opened the front door. He realized that she was not very mechanically minded and had not known quite how to invent the lock and was making a lot of pulls and clicks from memory, hoping he would not notice.

They went out into the street. The sun was rising (or seemed to be rising), and Smith Street looked much the same. He was not particularly surprised by the fact that, although it had been nighttime in the house, it should be daylight out of doors: Mildred, he remembered, was very good at this sort of thing. There was no one in sight, but he could hear kind Sid, their milkman (who played the clarinet in his spare time), clanging his bottles from the direction of Radnor Walk. The pub on the corner was shuttered, the iron tables forlorn and chairless in the early morning sunlight.

Ahead lay Burton Court, its tall trees still and feathery against a deep blue sky.

"Come along," said Mildred, hurrying. "I'm afraid it's rather late." She was walking her usual walk, a little stooped and busy, her thin legs twinkling. A strand of her grayish, pale golden hair had slid away from her bun. James followed her, still enjoying his toe-tip floating walk—rising with each light step and sailing through the air. One slightly sharper pressure on his toe brought him past her. "Oh, not now, James!" she exclaimed. "Walk properly, please! There may be people about. . . ." She seemed worried suddenly and, as he fell into step beside her, she said, "I should have worn a hat. Or one of those little veil things with bows. Not that I really like them, but one can slip them into one's handbag. I mean, for occasions like these. . . ."

But James was not listening: he was staring ahead at a cloud formation that had appeared rather suddenly above the treetops of Burton Court. It looked like a palace. In fact, it was a palace, rising turret upon turret, tier upon tier, from what—he guessed roughly—should have been the site of the Royal Hospital. The sun now seemed high in the sky, and the vast building, to James, looked too white and too shadowless, like something made of icing-sugar. He slowed his steps a little, guessing what they were in for: some of those "old fairy-tale people" again! After a while, on second thought, he cheered up slightly and quickened his step: sometimes these could be interesting.

There were halberdiers at the gate, where Mildred showed her pass and, in the courtyard, the usual golden-haired girl, playing with the usual golden ball, as he followed Mildred up the chalk-white marble stairs. There were halberdiers again outside the great doors, which stood open. There were two thrones, and some courtiers were murmuring together in the way they always did, but Mildred walked firmly through them, fanning herself with her pass, while James followed shyly behind.

Mildred turned left in the next corridor and then, with the happy gesture of one who knows herself to be welcome, threw open a pair of double doors. There was a burst of sunlight and the sound of voices. "Mildred! Dear Mildred!" someone cried out.

Mildred curtsied low and, past her shoulder, James could see the long room, the curly, golden furniture and the three middle-aged ladies grouped around the tea table. One rose as Mildred ran forward from her curtsy. There were kisses and embraces.

"Mildred, dear Mildred, who would remember us if you did not come?"

"This is James," said Mildred, breathless with pleasure. She turned and drew him forward. The large, pink-faced lady took James's hand and stared into his face wonderingly, almost questioningly.

"He prefers science fiction," confessed Mildred hurriedly, and the large lady's smile faded and she let go of James's hand. She sighed as she sat down, beckoning Mildred to a chair. "You know our dear Pumpkin, of course?"

"Yes, yes," said Mildred warmly. She rose to curtsy again. A black-haired lady, seated on a sofa, gently inclined her head. She had bright dark eyes and her smile, to James, seemed just a trifle mocking.

"And Belle, of course, you know?" said the large fair-haired lady as she gestured toward a card table.

"I know *of* her," said Mildred breathlessly. She curtsied a third time and then, a little shyly, sat down on the edge of her chair. "Of course I know *of* her."

The lady at the card table smiled stiffly and raised her lorgnette. She had a very straight back and her fox-colored hair was arranged in a fuzzy fringe. "So this then is Mildred?" she said. "The famous Mildred?"

"Poor dear Belle," said the fair lady, "lovely as ever, don't you think? But never sleeps, plays patience night and day."

"I suppose . . ." said Mildred. She hesitated. "I mean—it's only natural. When you come to think of it." As though to change the subject, she delved in her bag. "Look, I brought you these. I—I thought they might amuse you." She laid two magazines on the table beside the tea tray.

"How very kind," said the fair lady.

"Most kind," said the lady at the card table.

The dark lady called Pumpkin stretched out an arm and took a copy of *London at Large.* She settled back languidly into her corner and, putting her feet up, began to turn the pages.

"I do the piece at the end," explained Mildred, "the parties and things. . . ."

"How *very* clever," said the dark lady.

"It's *fun,*" said Mildred. "Such charming people, you know." She turned back again to the fair lady. "And how is dear Beau?" she asked eagerly.

"Well, very well." The large lady smiled and slightly shrugged her shoulders; her diamond necklace jangled musically as it overlapped her pearls. "We are none of us, of course, as young as we were."

"But he still enjoys a good day's fishing?"

"Yes, indeed."

"And his game of cribbage of an evening?"

"Yes, indeed. We all play cribbage."

"And you yourself, ma'am?"

"Boofy to you, dear Mildred. I am well. Very well."

James edged backwards toward a window. He felt very shy and out of place. But the fair lady had noticed his movement. She smiled at him kindly and leaned toward Mildred. "Perhaps," she said graciously, "James might like to play with Dulcibel in the courtyard?"

"No, no," said Mildred, "we mustn't stay. This is just a flying visit. How *is* dear Dulcibel?"

"Well, very well."

Mildred got up and moved across to the window. "Dear Dulcibel," she said, staring down at the courtyard. The fair lady came beside her. "No suitors, yet, of course?"

"Alas, no."

"She's very young still," said Mildred.

"Too young," said the fair lady sadly. She laid a hand on Mildred's arm. "Such an anxiety always . . . dear Mildred. I know you understand."

"Yes," said Mildred, "indeed I do." She hesitated tactfully. "You mean," she ventured at last, "that you still have the same trouble?"

"Yes, my dear." The fair lady sighed. "We don't talk about it."

"Isn't there *anything* you can do?"

"We've tried everything."

"Draining the well, for instance?"

"Oh, my dear, we've tried all that: it fills up almost as quickly as it empties. No, I'm afraid this is something that we just have to learn to live with."

"Someone told me—" said Mildred, "I can't quite remember who it was—something about a female of the species?"

"Ah, yes"—the fair lady sighed again—"at one time we pinned great hopes on that. But now we feel that story's just a rumor. Dear Beau was so good at organizing searches. He combed the whole kingdom—right up to Belungun-in-the-Marsh. . . ."

"A complete waste of time," remarked the dark lady from the sofa without looking up from her illustrated paper.

"Not altogether, dear, if you will forgive my saying so. He had some very good sport, dear thing: three brace of unicorn and a fire-eating dragon."

"Not fire-eating, dear—fire-breathing." She turned a page. "Lord and Lady Westcumberland have a very plain daughter."

"Oh," exclaimed Mildred, "Horatia. That picture doesn't really do her justice. She's a dear girl, really. Wonderful with horses."

"All the same," went on the fair lady indignantly, "for a man of Beau's age—"

"Oh, no one's denying Beau's a good marksman. But who, dear, I ask you—Belle and I were staying here at the time, you remember—wants an unrelieved diet of unicorn day after day? One might almost say week after week."

"I think Boofy's chef is wonderful with unicorn," said the lady at the card table.

"I can always recognize it," said the dark lady, turning over a page. Then she looked up at Mildred. "Why do you put in this bit about going to the hairdresser?"

"Because people are always asking me," said Mildred. "I have such a busy life, you see: they wonder how I fit it in."

"Ah, here's tea," said the lady at the card table. She gathered up her cards and began to shuffle them.

As the footmen entered with trays and cake stands, James moved up to Mildred and whispered in her ear. She laughed reprovingly and then she patted his hand. The fair lady caught her eye.

"James is longing to know," explained Mildred, "what you did with the dragon."

The fair lady looked very surprised. "The dragon? We threw it away of course. There's nothing you can do with a dragon. Not even the dogs would touch it."

"I'd have liked it," said James.

"No, dear, they're full of brimstone and goodness knows what else. And the skin cracks like pastry once it's dried—"

"A pity," said Mildred.

"Yes, yes. Dear Beau once thought of starting a small business: a cottage industry, you might term it—in the old days, of course, when there were more about—using the quills for arrows and curing the skins. But it didn't come to anything. And there was the storage difficulty."

"Of course," said Mildred.

"Have you ever seen a full-grown dragon? Really full-grown?"

"No," said Mildred, "as a matter of fact, I haven't. Not really full-grown," she added apologetically.

"Well, you must just take my word for it that a really fine adult specimen"—again the fair lady looked out of the window, screwing up her eyes—"is as long as that courtyard, with the pleached alley added. You see," she went on as James and Mildred came beside her, "what could poor Beau do with four of these creatures on his hands? And in hot weather, too."

"Yes, of course," said Mildred, "I see his problem. What bad luck. Such a good idea!"

"Yes, wasn't it? Poor Beau—and he was so keen, at first."

"Beau's keen on everything—at first," said the dark lady, who had moved behind the tea table. "Does Mildred take milk and sugar?"

"No tea, thanks!" exclaimed Mildred quickly. "We really mustn't stay. It has been wonderful . . . a great privilege, as always . . . *so* kind . . . and a real education for James."

"Must you really go?"

"Yes, we must. We have so much to get through."

The large, fair lady held onto Mildred's hand. "Dear Mildred, always so busy. And nobody forgotten. Where are you bound for now, I wonder?"

"Well, Much-Belungun—eventually."

"Much-Belungun-in-the-Marsh or Belungun-on-the-Hill?"

"Much-Belungun-under-Bluff," said Mildred.

The fair lady's eyes widened, and she held onto Mildred's hand even more tightly. "Oh, my dear Mildred, do you think you should? That's a very backward place."

"I find it rather quaint," said Mildred, smiling.

"Quaint? That's not the word I'd use. And to get there you'll have to go through the forest. Have you thought of that?" The pink face had become quite pale.

"Dear, kind Boofy. Please do not worry. I often go through the forest. It's all changed—since you were a girl: no witches—at least none to speak of—no goblins, no giants—"

"Are *all* the giants dead?" asked Belle in an interested voice, from the tea table.

"All," said Mildred, "and the forest is lovely at this time of the year."

"In that case," said the fair lady, "I suppose we must not dissuade you. You have your job to do."

"Yes," said Mildred, "Much-Belungun-in-the-Marsh, Much-Belungun-under-Bluff—it's all in a day's work to me."

"But please be careful, dearest Mildred."

"I will. I will. I am always careful. Come now, James, we must say good-bye."

As the large, fair lady took James's hand, she stared into his face, kindly but a little sadly. "Science fiction . . ." she murmured wonderingly.

Mildred walked briskly through the anteroom. She took no notice of the courtiers, some of whom glanced at them sideways and then, turning their backs, went on murmuring amongst themselves. James, very embarrassed, eyes fixed straight ahead, hurried to keep up with her. She looked happy and important, and something about her expression made James think there was a secret still to unfold. When they reached the dazzling brightness of the upper terrace, she turned quickly, taking hold of his arm.

"But you know *who* they are?" she said.

James shook his head, glancing uncomfortably at the halberdiers who he felt were well within earshot.

"Boofy and Beau were Beauty and Beast, you know—" She dropped her voice to an excited whisper. "The lady called Pumpkin was Cinderella. And Belle, of course—the lady playing cards—was the Sleeping Beauty."

"Oh," said James.

"And now you have seen them," Mildred went on in the same excited whisper, "you have actually seen them with your own eyes!" She paused. "Now very few people could say that, could they?"

James thought for a moment. "No, I suppose not," he said.

"And they're not the only ones, James, whom you're going to meet." She laughed happily. "You'll see! This may be rather exciting."

James was not so sure: sometimes things that had seemed "exciting" to Mildred did not always seem so to him. He looked at the landscape stretching away below the terrace: had it been there before? He supposed it must have been. It was rather like the background of an old Italian painting they had at home—not the original painting but a rather good reproduction. There was myrtle, heather, bracken, cypresses, pines; there were ravines and rocks; there were woods of oak and beech; in the distance there were mountains—he thought he could make out another castle, or was it a walled town? There were cloud shadows and sunlight. It was all very beautiful.

"Where are we exactly?" said James.

Mildred frowned slightly and followed the direction of his eyes. "It's hard to explain. I mean"—she hesitated—"you remember it said that they all 'lived happily ever after'?"

"But they're so old," said James.

"No, no," said Mildred, a little too sharply; "they're in their prime. They've gained by experience, and—" But she, too, looked a little puzzled and stared thoughtfully toward the distant mountains. "I suppose," she said after a moment, "you could call it The Land of Cockayne. . . ." She thought again, her brows still slightly wrinkled. "I don't see why not: it's a nice name. We mustn't be too literal, you see, James? And I suppose they do live on for ever and ever after—in the hearts of little children. . . ."

"They don't in mine," said James.

"Oh, James," exclaimed Mildred, now really impatient, "I don't know *anything* about science fiction! I can only take you where I *can* take you. You mustn't be ungrateful."

"I'm not. I mean—I just wanted to know where we are."

"Well, I've told you," said Mildred. "Come along now, dear, we've got a great deal to get through." And she made off toward the steps.

James came beside her. "What did she mean—that lady—about the forest?"

"It used to be dangerous," said Mildred.

"Isn't it now?"

"No, no, all that's changed ages ago. They don't always get things quite right—" She stopped suddenly. "That reminds me"—she fumbled in her satchel—"I forgot to leave them the article."

"What article?" asked James.

"Ah, here it is!" She drew out a small folder, glancing briefly at the contents. "It's just a little thing I write—to keep them in touch, you know. Yes, this is it. This will amuse them." She laughed as her eyes scanned the page. "The bit about Rapunzel's mother-in-law and Rapunzel dyeing her hair. Quite true but really rather funny." She started back toward the halberdiers.

"Couldn't I stay here?" asked James. He was not too keen on those courtiers in the first hall.

"Yes, if you like. I won't be long. Why don't you go down and play with Dulcibel?"

Left alone on the terrace, James stared about him. Beyond the balustrade, misty in the distance, he could see the forest. It lay in shadow, darkened by a cloud, but as he watched, the sun came out: the forest became green again and, beyond it, James could see a tall, white bluff. Some kind of cliff, it looked like, curving around as though to enclose a plateau. Very high, it must be, if he could see it from this distance. The mountains rose behind it, craggy and rather forbidding. That pile he had taken to be a castle might only be one of the crags. He hoped that Mildred would tell him more about this forest. He remembered that lady's face: it had looked very grave.

He walked to the edge of the terrace and leaned on the balustrade. It was warm from the sun, and immediately below him, beyond the lemon trees, he could see the princess playing with her golden ball beside the well. It was a large well; in fact, with its shallow curb, it looked more like a pond than a well, but he guessed it might be deep. As a game, the cup and ball looked rather fun, in a mild kind of way, and she was darting about very nimbly.

Rather shyly he moved along the balustrade toward the steps. He wondered if she spoke English. But of course she would: everybody did, on these trips he took with Mildred; it was one of the things she *could* manage.

As he went down the steps, the princess glanced up but went on playing. What was her name again? Dulcibel. Could he call her that? She went on with her game, even when he stood quite close beside her.

She was fair, with a large, high forehead, a tiny nose, and very long, light eyelashes—quite pretty really, in a dullish kind of way. Back and forth she ran, beside the well, a little breathlessly—tossing the chained ball in its golden cup. (It fitted exactly, James noticed.) She wore a little circlet of pearls on her wiry yellow hair. Her dress was cloth of gold and so too were her shoes.

"Don't you ever miss?" he asked at last.

She glanced at him sideways, blushing slightly, but went on tossing her ball. "Not often," she said, her eyes on the ball. "I get a lot of practice."

He watched her in silence a moment and then he said, "Could I have a go?"

"Well," she said, catching the ball in her hand and placing it back in the cup, "you've got to be careful."

"I would be," said James.

"Very careful," she went on. She held the ball and cup against her chest in a possessive kind of way.

"Why?" he asked.

"In case the chain broke and the ball fell into the water."

"Well, it's hollow, isn't it? We could fish it out again."

She smiled, a superior, rather sad little smile. "It's not so easy

as that. You see"—she hesitated, her eyes on his face—"there's a toad in that well."

"What difference does that make?"

"Or perhaps it's a frog. Come and look."

They peered down into the dank water, and at last he saw it, staring up at them with its striped eyes: it was sitting, bandy-armed, on a stone ledge.

"It's a toad," he remarked, after a moment.

"Well, whatever it is—if the chain broke and the ball fell into that well, he wouldn't give it back unless—" She dropped her voice suddenly and looked about her in a frightened kind of way.

"Unless what?"

"Unless I promised to marry him."

James stared at her incredulously, and then he looked again at the toad. It stared back at him stolidly, then blinked its catlike eyes.

"Are you sure?" he asked in an unbelieving voice.

"Yes," she said.

James was silent: there was something about that "Yes," spoken so simply, that had impressed him. "You'd think," he said at last, still staring into the well, "that he'd prefer another toad."

"That's just it!" exclaimed Dulcibel. She seemed very excited suddenly. "That's exactly it! How did you know?"

"Know what?" said James.

"That there was this toad—a very special kind—with a jewel in its head."

"I didn't know," said James.

"Well, there is. And he was very much in love with her."

Again James stared at the toad and the toad stared stolidly back: it did not look, to James, like a toad with a broken heart.

"What happened to this other toad then? Did it die?"

"No," exclaimed Dulcibel, "it can't die. It's magic." She sounded rather irritated. "I think someone's got her."

"Someone you know?"

"Not personally. You see, it's like this: all the witches are supposed to have fled—you know this, don't you?"

"I've heard it," said James.

"Except for one. They say she goes on and on. I've forgotten her name now. I used to know it." She wrinkled her forehead and thought for a moment. "Now, it seemed to me—and my parents thought this too—that if all the other witches are fled, or dead, or something, that this one witch must have something that keeps her safe. You see, if you have this toad, the one with a jewel, nothing can ever hurt you."

"You mean it's a talisman?"

"No, it *is* a toad," said Dulcibel, "and I think this witch has got it."

"But you don't know for certain?"

"No, nobody knows for certain."

"It may only be a rumor," said James.

Dulcibel sighed. "It may be." She moved nearer to the well to play with her cup and ball.

After Dulcibel's first few tosses, he went toward her. "Do you mind if I say something?"

She stopped playing and looked at him, rather surprised.

"No—I mean, it depends . . ."

"I was going to say," went on James, "that if I were you, I wouldn't play so close to the well."

"I never thought of that," said Dulcibel.

"It stands to reason."

"Yes, it does in a way"—vaguely she looked about her—"but over there, I'd get all tangled up in those lemon trees. And, besides, they're always full of bees. I might get stung. And I've always played here. I'm sort of used to it. . . ."

James looked at her rather sternly. "I think you do it on purpose just to make the game more exciting."

"Oh no," she faltered, "it isn't like that. You don't understand —you're from some other country. I—" Suddenly she broke off. Her eyes narrowed as she stared past his shoulder. "Who's this coming?"

James turned around. It was Mildred of course, looking rather pleased with herself and stuffing some papers into her satchel. She waved when she saw them, then began to draw on her gloves.

"What is she?" asked Dulcibel. She was looking rather scared.

"Just a person. Her name is Mildred. She visits people and writes things about them. For the papers, I suppose." Suddenly this seemed strange. For what papers? he wondered. And who published them? "Sometimes she takes me with her. She's very nice when you get to know her."

"Oh yes," said Dulcibel. She looked relieved as Mildred came closer. "I remember now. She's been here before."

"So you've made friends?" said Mildred happily as she came up beside them.

There was a little silence, as though neither knew quite what to reply. Dulcibel looked at James and James looked down at his foot, running the toe of his moccasin along a raised edge of the pavement. There had been something too wistful in Dulcibel's gaze: perhaps she had never had a friend?

Mildred was still talking. ". . . so much to get through," she was saying, "otherwise he could stay and play a little longer. Come, James, we must make our good-byes."

Dulcibel moved forward, and James put out his hand, but instead of taking it, she held out the cup and ball. "He hasn't had a turn yet," she explained to Mildred, but her eyes were on James's face. "You said you'd like one," and, as he seemed to hesitate, "Didn't you?"

"It's all right," said James uncomfortably; he saw she was trying to keep them, and—after all—it was a girl's game really.

"Very well," said Mildred, "have one little throw and then we must be off."

It took more than one little throw. This game, James realized, was very difficult. He wished they would not watch him, or that he could have practiced a little first. Once the ball flew back and hit him above the eye.

"Higher," said Dulcibel, "hold your arm higher."

He did so, a little impatiently, describing a great arc so that the ball flew out violently to the full length of the chain. A slender link gave way, and Dulcibel shrieked as the ball sailed away. Down it came with a piece of chain attached; they watched with anguished eyes as it banged and clattered across the paving stones. It fetched up, at last, beside the shallow coping of the well.

There was a deathlike silence. And then James said, "I'm terribly sorry," and went to retrieve the ball.

She took the toy without looking at him. Her face was very pale. "It doesn't matter," she said huskily as she examined the broken link. "We can get it mended. It's–it's done this before."

"I'm terribly sorry," said James again.

"The main thing is," said Mildred, "that it didn't fall into the water. You were a bit rough, James. But it was your first time. Anyway," she went on, "all's well that ends well."

She laughed then, a little apologetically: she had not meant to make a pun.

When they had made their good-byes, Dulcibel, still very pale, lingered at the top of the steps to watch them go down. They paused where the steps curved away for a final last wave. There she stood, the cupless ball hugged to her chest–very small, she looked, and somehow forlorn. Mildred blew her a kiss.

THREE

Once around the corner, Mildred hurried a little. "We've so much to get through," she said again (her thin legs vibrated a little as her heels clunked down on the stone). "Besides the Jacks, there may be a royal wedding and goodness knows what else—"

"What are the jacks?" asked James mechanically, and then he said, "Could I slide down this balustrade?"

"I don't see why not," Mildred began, and then she paused. "No, better not—someone's coming. . . ." She stood still, staring below. "It's Beau," she said, almost under her breath. She looked rather shy suddenly. "Boofy's husband. You remember—he used to be the Beast?" She laid a hand on James's arm. "We must stand aside," she whispered.

The stout gentleman approaching up the steps was taking them slowly. He was panting a little. Slung over his shoulders—like a golf bag—was a quiver full of arrows. In his right hand he carried a bow. The rest of his dress—the lace, the ruffles, the embroidered waistcoat—seemed vaguely eighteenth century (just as Boofy's, James remembered, had seemed vaguely Edwardian). As he came abreast of them, Mildred curtsied. "How good to see you, sir!"

The stout gentleman, not sorry to pause, stared at her blankly with pale gray, fishlike eyes. He held out the fingers of his left hand, which Mildred took, hurriedly and shyly. "And looking so well," she added, dropping the limp hand.

"Fair, fair," said the stout gentleman, still staring. James thought perhaps he did not recognize Mildred. Mildred herself seemed a little uncertain.

"Perhaps, sir, you do not remember me," she said. "They call me Mildred. I—I bring the news, the papers. . . ."

"Ah, yes," said the stout gentleman, "indeed."

"I've left your copy, sir, of *Field and Gun.*"

"Most kind," said the stout gentleman, looking beyond Mildred as though calculating in his tired way how many more steps there were still to climb.

"And *The Amateur Archer,*" said Mildred.

There was a sudden gleam in the fishlike eyes, the dawning of recognition. "Ah, yes, indeed—you are Mildred?" Now on the large red face James saw the beginnings of a smile. "Most kind. Most kind. And how do you find yourself?"

Mildred blushed. "Well, sir. I thank you."

James was impressed by the "I thank you"; it sounded so right, somehow. He looked at Mildred with renewed respect—how good she was with these people!

The stout gentleman bowed slightly and raised his limp left hand rather wearily in a gesture of farewell. Mildred curtsied, turning toward him as he went on up the stairs. She wobbled slightly but recovered quickly by grasping the balustrade. She was smiling happily and gazing upward. James was relieved that she did not move: he had thought for a moment that, out of respect, they might have had to walk backwards down the stairs—not easy for Mildred in those teetering, high-heeled shoes.

As the stout gentleman, turning the corner of the stairs, disappeared from view, James said, "What period are we in?"

"Period?" repeated Mildred vaguely. "Oh, I see what you mean: you're thinking of his clothes. These people, James—if you can understand—belong to no particular period: they belong—as one might say—to Time Immemorial. They wear more or less what they like. In some cases, of course, they go by the illustrator. . . ."

Mildred turned and began to descend the steps. She was delving in her satchel. "I have the key to the postern gate. We'll go out that way. . . ." It was a very large key, James saw, as they pottered down the steps, and she dangled it on her finger. "Not many people know about the postern gate."

At the foot of the steps, instead of going forward into the laid-out, formal gardens, Mildred turned left into what had once been a pleached alley. Nowadays, the branches met overhead in a pleasant, untidy abandon; there was moss on the path and nettles in the shadows. Little blobs of sunlight trembled on the stones. It was a nice, mysterious kind of place. After a few twists and turns, they came to a wall—a high stone wall, overhung with ivy. A bed of ferocious-looking nettles reached up toward the dark green fronds above.

"Oh dear!" exclaimed Mildred, staring unhappily.

"Where's the postern gate?" asked James.

"Behind all that," said Mildred. "It can't have been used for years. . . ."

James thought for a moment. His moccasins were of leather and his red pajamas fairly thick. "I'll tread down the nettles," he said. "Lend me your satchel." He thrashed about with Mildred's satchel, knocking the plants down from right to left, and then bravely he trampled upon them with occasional "Ahs" and "Ouches." He drew back the fronds of ivy, interlacing one with another and, at last, the door stood revealed.

It was a very old door, heavily barred and studded. Some of the wood looked wet and mildewed, some was stained with moss. The top of the arch rose to a point. It was exactly like any postern gate James had ever imagined.

"Thank you, James," said Mildred nervously, making her way across the prostrate nettles. "That was very clever. Ouch!" she exclaimed as a stray leaf brushed her shin. She stood on one leg and rubbed her stocking, grasping the ring in the door. Straining, she turned the ring, and the latch lifted squeakily and fell again with a clatter. The keyhole below the ring seemed filled with dirt and moss. "It's locked all right," she said.

They scraped it out with a twig and then pushed the twig right through. James put his eye to the hole. "I can see sunlight," he said.

The key slid in quite loosely, but it took some time to turn it; at last, it gave way with a grind. Mildred tried the ring again, and the latch rose up grumpily. "Pull, James!" cried Mildred, and the door opened suddenly, scraping its base across the nettles. There was a burst of brilliant sunshine. They fell back a pace or two, staring out at the countryside.

"Marvelous," said Mildred. "Thank you, James. I could never have managed it alone."

FOUR

Before them lay a very pleasant view, some sort of common land, tree-fringed at the edges, with the mountains rising behind. Gorse grew here and clumps of heather. A sandy cart track stretched away in front of them between low bracken-covered banks. Here and there wild rose bushes were interlaced with honeysuckle. There was a peaty smell in the air.

James liked this place: it was more a boy's kind of place. He ran up a bank and gazed about. "Where did you say we were going?"

"To Much-Belungun-under-Bluff," said Mildred. "There's something there I'd like to see for myself. Since I was last there, there have been rumors . . . all nonsense, no doubt. But we do have to go through the forest," she added, as though to change the subject.

"What sort of rumors?" asked James, intrigued.

"Just rumors," replied Mildred lightly. "I have my job, you see, James, and my job is to report. And accurately, you know. Come along now. We'd better get going."

James ran up on the bank while Mildred kept to the track. Some goats were grazing under a hawthorn bush whose branches were stripped of leaves. A little girl sat on a lichen-covered rock. She wore a red skirt and a small black bodice. She stared at James as he passed, and James stared back. The girl smiled.

"Who's that?" he asked Mildred as they went on by.

"I don't know everybody, James. Just some goatherd or other. We'll see a lot of these people—shepherds and goatherds and swineherds and woodcutters and charcoal-burners and all sorts. They're not very interesting. At least, not to write about. If you look back now, you can still see the palace."

James turned. Yes, there it was within its encircling walls—tier upon tier of glistening turrets and terraces. Surrounded now by this quiet green countryside, it looked less like a wedding cake and more like a dwelling place—albeit rather a large one. But that was what always happened, he remembered, on these outings with Mildred: things that seemed strange at first, and somehow false, gradually became quite real.

"Must have cost a pretty penny to build," he said.

"Look!" exclaimed Mildred. "There's Dulcibel! There on the topmost terrace—just below that pinnacle!"

James screwed up his eyes and could just perceive a hint of movement beyond the balustrade. What seemingly endless flights of stairs she must have tackled to reach that dizzy height.

"Look," said Mildred again, "you can see the gold of her dress. Wave to her, James."

"She couldn't see from there."

"Wave all the same."

James waved.

"Poor child," said Mildred as they resumed their walk, "she's far too much alone, but they don't seem to see it somehow."

They walked on in silence for a while. Then Mildred said, "Of course, it's all nonsense about that toad."

"How do you mean?" said James. Suddenly interested, he clambered down from the bank and came beside her.

"Well, dear, everybody knows it turns into a prince."

"*They* don't," said James.

"It's not for want of my telling them. I just can't convince them. I've given up trying now."

"But are you *sure*?" asked James.

"Of course, I'm sure. I know the whole story. As you should," she added, "if you weren't so keen on science fiction."

"It may not be the same toad," said James.

"But it must be," argued Mildred. "The bad fairy at her christening, the golden cup and ball—everything points to it."

James did not reply for a moment. "All I can say," he announced at last, "is that if I were Dulcibel, I wouldn't bank on it."

They walked on in silence for a while, and when, at last, they came within the shade of the trees, the sunlight fell on the ground in uneven patches of warmth, surrounded by darker shadows. The stones were moss-covered, and the bracken around them now rose to the height of a man. There was no wind. The branches above them hung motionless, and as they walked, dead twigs cracked harshly beneath their feet. There was a dark, rich smell.

"Are there wolves in this forest?" asked James.

"Oh, please, James!" said Mildred.

"But are there?" he persisted.

"Bound to be. But I try not to think of wolves. Really, James, we were enjoying ourselves. . . ."

"I like to think of wolves," said James.

The cart track wound on and on, turning and twisting, until at last they came to a glade. It was a bright place, warm and gay with sunshine. On one side of the cart track the land fell away to a stream.

"We'll rest here a minute," said Mildred. She took out her notebook and sat down on a fallen tree, quite dead now and bleached by the sun and rain. It lay with silvery roots exposed, and James wondered idly, as he made his way to the stream, what freak kind of tempest could have wrenched it out of the ground, here in this sheltered spot.

The stream was full of little waterfalls, running from pool to pool. There were ferns on the banks, and dark under a rock he thought he saw the shadow of a fish.

Mildred, on her tree trunk, was scribbling away. Sometimes she would pause and smile, tapping her teeth with her pen and staring into space. She looked very happy.

After a while, James kicked off his slippers and waded into the stream. The water purled and rippled over his bare toes, and it was all very pleasant and refreshing. This, he thought, might turn out to be one of Mildred's happier inspirations: if it was she who had invented this forest, she had invented it very well. After a while, he decided to dam the pools with stones and alter the course of the water. He did this for some time, and then another idea occurred to him. He rolled his pajama trousers high on his thighs, and wading across to the opposite bank, he started lifting stones—heavy stones, furry with dried, tough moss and with muddy caves between them.

"What are you doing, James?" called Mildred. She was putting away her notebook.

"Looking for toads," he said.

Mildred got up and came toward him. She watched him for a moment and then she said, "It isn't any good, James."

"You never know," said James, parting a clump of maidenhair. "If we found a lady toad, he *might* just take to her."

Mildred smiled. "Instead of Dulcibel?"

"Something like that. We could try."

"It's no good, James. They've tried everything—those people up at the palace. There's nothing they haven't tried. It's a spell, you see. And not a bad spell either—as I keep on telling them—if it turns out all right in the end."

"Supposing it doesn't? What then?"

"James, dear James, it is very pleasant to come and visit these people—and they like it—but one must never become too involved in their lives: it always leads to trouble. They must go on as they have always gone on. Put on your slippers now, dear. And tidy yourself up a bit. There isn't much farther to go."

She turned away toward the cart track, and James followed her reluctantly: he could have stayed in this place all day.

They walked in silence for a while, and then Mildred said, "All the same, it was very kind and thoughtful of you."

The path had darkened again. Beams of sunlight sloped down through the shadows ahead, making some molten pools. Suddenly James stood still. An old oak stood at a turn of the path, blasted and twisted as though by lightning. Nailed to the bark, joined by a piece of bone, was a pair of bull's horns, stained and weather-beaten. A whitish object dangled below them; to this was tied a bunch of wilted herbs. By the tree's roots a narrow, muddy track led away among the brambles into the darkness.

"What's that thing?" he asked.

Mildred glanced briefly at the horns, and then she looked away again. "It's a charm," she said shortly. "Big Hans put it up."

"Who's he?"

"Oh, come, James. You must have heard of Big Hans and Little Hans."

A memory came back to James of a room in his grandmother's house, a small room, filled with books and sunlight. There had often been a patch of sunlight on the carpet, behind a large armchair that stood with its back to the window. That was where he would sit and read, his back against the shutters. A secret place. He remembered the dusty, fusty smell of the old book and the carpety smell of the carpet. It was a book that had belonged to his grandmother as a child. Some of the pages were missing. Yes, he remembered Big Hans and Little Hans. But he could not remember the story. He looked again at the charm. "What's it for?" he asked.

"To keep off the evil eye or some such nonsense. That's the way to Hecubenna's house."

"Who's he?"

"She. She's a witch. Or was. I don't suppose she's there now."

Mildred walked on rather hurriedly. James, lagging behind, plucked a stalk of grass and began to chew it. He was thinking of witches and of what Dulcibel had said. That path beside the oak tree had looked well worn.

FIVE

The track began to widen after a while and the trees to become sparse. Between these, every now and again, they would see a hut or a space where woodcutters had been at work. Then, at last, the trees thinned right away: they were on common land again, and there before them lay a huddle of houses.

"This," said Mildred, "is Much-Belungun-under-Bluff." And the Bluff was there, a crumbling grayish white, towering above the village, toward which it seemed to lean. Very menacing, it looked. If that crashed down, thought James, it would bury all those houses. And it was a pretty village, grouped around a green with a pump. Most of the houses were thatched, clean, and whitewashed between their darkened beams. There was a pond with ducks, two tethered goats, and an old sow, asleep in the sun, against a lichened wall.

As they approached, there was a smell of fresh manure, of a ham cooking with herbs, and the spicy smell of wallflowers. "Quaint, isn't it?" said Mildred. "*So* old world. I hope your mother won't mind, James, if we're a little bit, well—Bohemian: we're going to stay at the pub." This did not seem at all "Bohemian" to James: his mother liked pubs very much, especially country ones, and so did his father. He rather liked them himself: they meant potato chips and Coca-Cola and sitting outside in the sun. And there were always other children doing just the same. And, on the way home to luncheon, the grownups were always affable and full of jokes, and suddenly inclined to spoil.

"Oh, good!" he said.

"Well, this is rather a special pub," went on Mildred as they approached a long, low whitewashed building. "It is kept by two very famous people. But," she added, "you'll find them quite unspoiled, I'm glad to say."

There were benches against the whitewashed wall and flowerpots on the windowsills. It was all very neat and gay. What was it called? he wondered. And as Mildred went on through the dark doorway, he stepped back to look at the sign. It was blank. It hung there on its iron support above the lintel, barely stirring in the calm air. Funny, thought James, as he followed Mildred inside—a pub without a name.

"Anyone at home?" called Mildred, peering into the dimness.

There was a scrape of chair legs on the stone floor and a voice said, "Well, I never!" A gaunt old man appeared, neatly dressed in a leather jacket over a spotless shirt. He was very tall and smiling happily. "Well, I never!" he said again. "Jack!" he called, looking back into the room. "Come you here and see who's come!"

"Dear Jack," said Mildred, taking his gnarled hands, "how well you look! How have you both been keeping?"

"I'm not complaining," said the old man, and he called again over his shoulder, "Jack boy, come you here!"

Another old man emerged from the shadows. He was shorter and fatter and redder in the face. Were they both called Jack? James wondered. Evidently they were because Mildred took his hands, too, and said, "Dear Jack, how good to see you!"

James glanced swiftly about the room, the spotless stone floor, the trestle tables, the great casks of ale. There was a fire in the stone fireplace, with various cooking pots simmering gently on the neatly leveled embers. There was a savory hamlike smell. James suddenly felt hungry.

"And this is James," Mildred was saying. She drew him forward. James put out his hand to the tall old man, who took it kindly between his own. "And this, James," went on Mildred, "is Jack–" She paused as though to give full effect to her next words. "Jack-the-Giant-Killer."

"Oh!" gasped James. He was amazed.

"And this other dear Jack," said Mildred warmly, "is Jack-of-the-Beanstalk. Another giant-killer, too, one might say."

"I never took it up like he did," said the smaller old man as he took James's hand.

"Now don't be modest," said Mildred. "You did very well. You know you did."

"For an amateur," said the old man, and he sighed.

"And look what you grow in the garden! It's quite marvelous."

"I grows it and he cooks it," said Jack-of-the-Beanstalk.

"And how well he cooks it," said Mildred, "don't I remember!"

"Now come you in and sit," said Jack-the-Giant-Killer. He drew two stools from under the trestle table and set them beside the fire. He blew on both before he would let them be seated, fearing a trace of ash. "Can't keep a thing decent around here," he grumbled.

No sooner had they sat down than Jack-the-Giant-Killer was up again. He seized a broom from beside the chimney, shouting, "Out! Out! I won't have ye in here!"

James, leaning sideways from his seat, saw two small objects dancing on the flagstones. Quivering, scarlet toadstools, they looked like. He peered more closely. No, not toadstools: they looked like (but how could they be?) a pair of scarlet slippers.

"Out! Out!" cried the old man, sweeping at them with the broom. They danced out backwards, heels toward the door. Their quick, darting movements seemed to have faltered a little. The old man swept them across the threshold, and then he shut the door. "Bringing in the dirt," he grumbled as he set the broom back

in its place. "Leave that door open for ten minutes, and in they come."

Jack-of-the-Beanstalk took his pipe from his mouth. "Not as often as all that," he said mildly.

Mildred had become rather pale. "I thought," she said, her voice a little shaky, "I thought—correct me if I am wrong—that, in the story, you know—that the shoes used to have feet in them?"

"They did have feet in them at one time," said Jack-the-Giant-Killer, "but it was the shoes that danced."

Jack-of-the-Beanstalk, at the far side of the fire, blew out a curl of smoke. "When they come in like that," he said thoughtfully, "very quick and all of a sudden like, seems to me always that they want to tell you something. . . ."

"Well, they can tell it to me outside," said Jack-the-Giant-Killer. He, too, took a clay pipe from a jar on the chimney beam and began to fill it. Taking a seat on the stone slab beside the hearth, he stretched out his long legs. He smiled at James, jerking his head sideways toward the farther wall. "Like to look at those?"

"Now he's off," murmured Jack-of-the-Beanstalk.

James got up and went to the wall. A curious row of objects hung there in a line above the wainscot: they looked like some kind of old-fashioned fly whisks made of hair with wooden handles from which they hung.

"What are they?" he asked.

Jack-the-Giant-Killer laughed and drew on his pipe, "Aha—that would be telling."

"He'll tell you soon enough," said Jack-of-the-Beanstalk.

"Count them," said Jack-the-Giant-Killer. He was smiling happily and prodding down the tobacco in his pipe. James counted them. "There are thirteen," he said.

"That's right. Eight giants, three giantesses, and a couple of ogres."

"One ogre," muttered Jack-of-the-Beanstalk.

"Always kept a lock of their hair," said Jack-the-Giant-Killer. "You won't see anything like that again in a hurry. Thirteen variegated tresses of genuine giants' hair."

"Twelve and a horse's tail," muttered Jack-of-the-Beanstalk, speaking into the fire. He got up suddenly and lifted the lid of a cooking pot. "This will be mush in a moment."

Jack-the-Giant-Killer swung around. "You leave that pot alone," he said. "I got it just where I want it." He turned to James. "You hungry?" he asked.

"I am a bit," said James.

"And it does smell good," put in Mildred quickly.

"Right then. We'll eat now and talk afterwards." All the same, he could not resist picking up a dark gray tress and sliding it through his fingers. "This old fellow now. He led me a dance and no mistake. Once or twice—and I don't mind admitting it—I thought I'd lost him. In the end, though, I got round to his rear like—" He dropped the tress suddenly and turned toward the hearth. "Anyhow, I'll tell you afterwards"—he glared at the back of Jack-of-the-Beanstalk, who had begun to set the table—"when we're *quiet.*"

The scrubbed table was soon laid out with wooden bowls, wooden spoons, and two-pronged wooden forks. There was a salad of lettuce hearts, sorrel, chives, and marjoram. Big Jack set the casserole before Mildred and lifted the lid: the smell was so delicious that Mildred caught her breath. "What can it be?" she murmured happily, taking up the ladle.

"It" was broad beans—but such as James had never tasted before. Brownish olive with gentle braising, and swimming in some juice not quite their own: tasty lumps of smoked sausage, transparent cubes of crispy pork fat, and another flavor, sharp and delicate. "Fresh coriander," Big Jack told them, "you can't beat it—not with beans." There was mead or ale. James chose mead. ("Gently James," warned Mildred, "it's very strong.") After that was sheep's cheese, butter, and crusty whole-meal bread. For James, there were comfits of sugared marrow scattered with aniseed. He did not like those quite as much.

"But tell me," said Mildred, feeling in her bag for her handkerchief, "the village seems very quiet today. Where is everybody?" Delicately, she dabbed her mouth.

"All gone to the marriage of a king's daughter," said Jack-of-the-Beanstalk.

"Oh, really!" Mildred became suddenly animated. "I ought to look in on that. Which king?"

"We don't rightly know which king: this land's got so full of kingdoms, and kings, and what not, you just can't keep pace with them nowadays. And what's more, they all seem to have this one beautiful daughter, with the natural result—as you might say—that there aren't enough princes to go around: they all end up marrying swineherds, or woodcutters, or the seventh son of some poor blacksmith. We just don't go any more."

"That's a pity," said Mildred. "I mean surely you'd enjoy the banquet in the courtyard, the music, the colored lanterns, the dancing . . . ?"

"The banquet in the courtyard!" exclaimed Jack-of-the-Beanstalk. "You just can't get near the banquet in the courtyard: people are setting out four and five days in advance, taking their bedding and cooking pots and camping around the palace. . . . Roads all blocked . . . nothing moving for miles. No, thank you. Not for us. We prefer a bit of peace in our own back garden. And what's more," he went on, "in the old days that banquet was meant to last a week: now, they tell me, every crumb's gone in the first half hour."

"Oh dear," said Mildred, "I'm so sorry—it used not to be like that: times, I suppose, are changing everywhere. All the same," she went on, "I think I ought to go. It's my job, you see, and I've always got my pass."

"You must please yourself, ma'am," said Jack-of-the-Beanstalk. He leaned across the table suddenly, smiling at James. "You enjoyed them beans?" he said. And, as James nodded happily, he went on, "Take a look at that!" He was pointing to a large glass case above the chimney piece.

James twisted around. It was several feet long, the kind of case in which he had often seen stuffed fish. It contained a large kidney-shaped object, burnished dark brown. "What about that for a bean?" asked the old man.

James got up and walked toward it. "A bean?"

"That's what it is. One of the beans from the original beanstalk!" He got up, too, and went toward the chimney and took up his pipe. "The one that came up in a night. . . ."

"Now he's off!" growled Jack-the-Giant-Killer and began rather noisily to clear the table, clashing the wooden porringers together and stamping back and forth on the flagstones.

"Can I help you?" asked Mildred, quickly rising from the table.

"No, ma'am," put in Jack-of-the-Beanstalk, speaking loudly from the hearth, "he's no *call* to do it. A widder-woman comes." He turned back to James, filling his pipe, and went on. "Mind you, that first bean I planted wasn't half that size. Not a tenth even. But I've always been one for a nice bit of compost—"

"Do forgive me," interrupted Mildred. She went up to Jack-of-the-Beanstalk and laid an apologetic hand on his arm. "But if I'm going to go to this wedding, I think perhaps I had better get started. Is there any kind of conveyance?"

"Conveyance?" repeated Jack-of-the-Beanstalk, still caught up in memories of the past.

"To take me to this kingdom. A carrier or something? Does Little Hans still function?"

"Little Hans went by not a moment agone," said Jack-the-Giant-Killer, "with a load of grain for the miller."

"Oh, that's splendid!" cried Mildred. "I can find him at the mill. Do you want to come, James?"

James looked from Mildred's to the faces of the two old men. They looked back at him questioningly, smiling their welcome. He hesitated. Sometimes, on these trips, he felt it safer to stay near Mildred: Mildred, as you might say, "knew the ropes." And yet? He looked back again at the smiling, uncertain faces. "I'd like to stay here," he said.

There was a short silence. Mildred turned to the old men, looking from one to the other. "Are you sure? I know it's an inn, but a child on his own. . . . I mean, it wouldn't be too much for you?"

"He can stay as long as he likes," said Jack-of-the-Beanstalk.

"As long as he likes," echoed Jack-the-Giant-Killer, and humming to himself in a rather tuneless way, he carried the dishes out into the scullery. Jack-of-the-Beanstalk went over to the case on the wall and examined his bean. Both old men seemed delighted.

James took hold of Mildred's sleeve. "You'll be coming back tonight?" he asked her, keeping his voice rather low.

"That's just it, James. I hope so. But on these occasions, one just cannot be sure."

James glanced toward Jack-of-the-Beanstalk. He had opened the case and was passing his hand lovingly over the surface of the bean.

"But what about my mother?" he said hurriedly to Mildred. "Tomorrow morning. I mean—"

Mildred laughed, but she too lowered her voice. "Time here isn't like time there. We could stay here six weeks, and it would still be tomorrow morning when you wake in bed at home. I've told you that many a time."

"But are you certain?" James persisted.

Mildred laughed again—very reassuringly. "As sure as I am that that frog will turn into a prince if they'd only believe it!"

"It's a toad," muttered James.

"Oh, well—whatever it is. Now where did I put my gloves, I wonder?"

James looked about him in a vague kind of way while Mildred delved into her bag. She drew out her notebook, her pass, two magazines, a case with her glasses, a handkerchief, and—last—a key. "Oh, James—" she said.

"What is it?"

"We never relocked the postern gate!"

"Didn't we?"

"No. It all comes back to me—I remember unlocking it. Then we went through. Then we turned back and pulled it to. It shut with a clang, I remember. Oh dear, how very stupid—I must have been thinking of my own front door!"

"Does it matter?" asked James.

"It might matter," said Mildred unhappily.

"Would these be yours?" asked Jack-the-Giant-Killer. He had come back from the scullery, Mildred's gloves in his hand. "Found 'em on the tray."

"Ah, yes, indeed," said Mildred. "Thank you so very much. And for the lovely luncheon, and for everything. And you'll be good, James, won't you? I hope I won't be long. I may not even stay for the banquet: it is really only to take a note of who's there. . . ."

The two Jacks moved forward to help her, but she opened the door herself. "Such a dear old latch," she said. As the door swung open, the little red shoes danced in again. "Oh dear!" exclaimed Mildred. "I *am* so sorry! I never thought they'd be waiting outside—"

"Out! Out!" cried Jack-the-Giant-Killer, running for the broom. The little red shoes danced lightly under a table. The broom came after them, but they swerved nimbly behind one of the trestles, marked time under a stool for a moment, and then came darting up to James. James moved back—not afraid exactly, but a little startled.

"Out! Out!" shouted the old man with wide sweeps of the broom. "Little varmints! Out you go!" This time he actually swept them over the threshold, and they tumbled over each other in a protesting kind of way.

Mildred, outside, was still apologizing. Then she called out good-bye as the old man shut the door. "Good-bye and thank you," they could hear her say.

"Dratted little creatures!" said Jack-the-Giant-Killer as he set the broom back in its place. He sat down heavily and wiped his brow with his sleeve. "Fair wear you out, those ones do."

Jack-of-the-Beanstalk had closed the glass case and, sucking his pipe, was staring through the window. "I still say," he remarked thoughtfully, after a moment, "when they come running in like that, sudden like, that they've something to tell you." He looked around at James and waved his pipe toward the window. " 'Tis a lovely afternoon. Care for a turn?" he said.

The Green glowed richly in the late sunshine, but the shadows were getting longer. James looked around him quickly: there was no sign of the little red shoes. There was only one person in sight—an old woman in a wimple filling her pitcher at the pump. They made their way across the Green to the scattered huddle of houses. The cobbled lanes were strangely empty and most of the houses shuttered. They called on the miller to inquire about Mildred. White with flour, he shouted down from his grain loft. Yes, she had caught Little Hans just in time, and in spite of the other passengers, there had been room for her in the cart. "Don't envy her that journey," he said as he turned away into the shadows. Then he turned back again to add that she had seemed "spry enough."

James looked toward the Bluff. It was farther away than he had thought, perhaps because it was even higher than at first he had imagined—a towering, leaning mass that seemed to threaten the village. "Not much of a place that," said Jack-of-the-Beanstalk.

"I'd like to see it closer," said James.

"The closer you get, the less you'll see," said Jack. "Hangs over like. Stretches away for miles, they say, on top—right up into the mountains. Quite a kingdom, as you might say." He paused and, feeling in his pouch-like pocket, drew out his pipe and began to fill it thoughtfully. "We don't bother with it," he said after a moment.

"Has anybody ever climbed it?"

"Climbed *that!*" snorted the old man. "And who would want to?" He seemed a little troubled.

James still stared, fascinated by that awful, craggy face of leaning rock. "What's that dark mound—there at the foot of it?"

The old man did not look up from his pipe. "A lot of old muck," he said.

"What kind of muck?" asked James.

"Muck! Just muck," the old man snapped. He sat down suddenly on the edge of an old horse trough. James sat down beside him. Still staring at the Bluff, James—who was a keen rock-climber—said, "But if you had ropes and crampons and the right sort of boots and—"

The old man turned on him suddenly. "Now look you here, we don't none of us talk about that Bluff. We don't none of us talk about it."

"Why ever not?" asked James.

"Least of all afront of Jack. Least of all afront of him. Not a word, in our house—say Jack's in the room—do you say about that Bluff. You speak of that Bluff and you'll upset him—you'll upset him something terrible."

James was silent for a moment. "I wish I knew why," he said at last. His voice sounded troubled.

"Everybody knows why. That's to say, all those in Much-Belungun-under-Bluff. Among ourselves like." His breathing had become quite fast. "Beyond that, we don't say nothing."

On the way home, they talked of beans and beanstalks and other harmless topics. They spoke of tilling and planting and the phases of the moon; of frost and drought and the mysteries of the soil. They passed the miller's son, a tall, fair lad, as dusty as his father. He was leading a mule laden with sacks of grain. Jack bade him good evening, but he did not reply. "Never speaks, that one, except to animals," explained old Jack. "Shy like, but I keep on trying. . . ."

By the time they reached the inn again, James felt he had learned many things, and old Jack had become lighthearted again.

After supper (of cabbage soup and delicious mutton pies) the talk turned to giants. James was enthralled, but Jack-of-the-Beanstalk yawned loudly and took himself off to bed. "It's been a long day," he said to James, "what with the digging in the morning."

"Digging and muck—that's all he ever thinks about," said Jack-the-Giant-Killer. "Well, that was my third giant," he went on, concluding his present story. "Now, this fellow here"—crossing the room, he unhooked the fourth tress from the wall—"was a different kettle of fish altogether. . . ." And he laid out the tress beside the three others on the table.

James listened, spellbound. Now and again he would ask a question and, unlike Jack-of-the-Beanstalk, the Giant-Killer answered it fully. There was no detail he did not remember, no sly trick he could not recall. His face was alive and happy, reliving the dangers of his past. After the twelfth giant, he got up from his seat and went over to bank up the fire. He said it was time for bed.

"Oh, do go on," begged James. "Just tell me about this last one!"

"Nay, 'tis past midnight," said old Jack. Suddenly, he looked very weary: the light had gone from his face and his shoulders seemed to droop. All the same, he looked across the room at the thirteenth tress. In fact, he almost seemed to glare at it. He shook his head slowly. "Nay," he said again and, turning away, took up a candle. " 'Tis time for bed now."

A little bed had been made up for James in a ground-floor room, which was full of apples: apples on the windowsill, apples on the chests, apples on the open shelves of the closet. Dried herbs and onions hung from the ceiling. The bed was of the kind he thought was called a truckle bed. He sat down on it and felt himself sink into a feather mattress. Old Jack went past him, candle in hand, and closed the lattice window.

"Don't bother," said James, "I like it open."

"You can't have it open. Not at night," said old Jack. He was making fast the latch. "Because of the hobgoblins," he added, coming back to the bed. He set the candle in its pewter holder on a stool at the head. "There's a crevice yonder"—he jerked his head, and James guessed that he meant the Bluff—"that's full of 'em."

"What do they do to you?" asked James after a moment. He looked rather uneasy.

"They don't do nothing to you. But you don't want them in the house. Now sleep you well," he said, "and careful of the light."

James sat on the edge of his bed for quite a long time, thoughtfully eating apples.

SEVEN

The next morning, when James went in to breakfast, Mildred had still not returned. The old men did not seem worried. "It's the traffic on the road," explained Jack-the-Giant-Killer. "There's no one come back as yet." He was preparing eggs for James at the hearth: a lump of butter in a shallow earthenware dish, gently guided to the outside rim of the ashes. There were other kinds of pots, some nearer to the red heart of the fire, one above it hanging on a hook, others set about in varying positions according to the heat required. On this open hearth, James realized, Jack could grill, stew, roast, fry, and bake. A large wooden box contained a pile of brushwood, which he used as delicately as a painter uses a palette —to vary degrees of heat. On the table was honey in the comb, curds and whey, some kind of drop scones, cream and a large bowl of fresh raspberries. The old men had already eaten: James had overslept.

Now he overate. The sun was pouring in through the latticed windows; he could hear "the widder-woman" clattering about in the scullery and a cow lowing in the field behind. Then the old men left him: big, tall Jack to tend the animals; small, round Jack to weed his garden. "Get out of it!" growled Jack-the-Giant-Killer as he opened the door and fumbled with his foot at something on the threshold. "Out, I say! Out!" He slammed the door to after him, and James, hastily mopping up his eggs, knew the little red shoes had come back again.

He carried his used dishes into the scullery where "the widder-woman," rosy as the apples in his bedroom, bid him good day and said that there was "no call for it." "And what will ye be doing with yourself this fine morning," she went on, "with everybody gone to the wedding?"

"Oh, I'll mess about," said James and, smiling rather shyly, retired again to the bar room. He knew what he wanted to do; he wanted to go and examine that crevice. What were hobgoblins, he wondered, and did they only come out at night? "I'll take a stick," he thought, and chose a long thumb stick made of hawthorn with a forked end from the many others stuck upright in a barrel. He opened the door very gingerly to keep out the little red shoes.

He need not have worried. They danced away from him—in a dance of delight, it seemed—with their toes pointed toward him. Dancing away backwards, as though enticing him to follow. He remembered the words of Jack-of-the-Beanstalk: had they really, perhaps, come to tell him something? Or to take him somewhere? What could they be wanting? he wondered. And was it good news or bad? There was no harm, he decided suddenly, in warily trying them out. He closed the door very carefully and, turning, came toward them.

They danced with joy. It was a pretty dance, heel and toe, with figures in it; and then they twisted away and ran ahead of him. He followed casually, pretending not to notice them.

They led him across the green toward the forest lane, the lane through which he had come with Mildred (was it really only yesterday?). Steadily now they tripped ahead, giving—now and again—a sudden, satisfied skip.

It was good to be out of doors again. He remembered with sudden pleasure the clearing by the stream, the dams he had built, the little waterfalls. He quickened his step. He felt he wanted to run: to catch up with the shoes, perhaps to pass them. But when he tried it, they were too quick for him. Sometimes they seemed to wait for him, marking time. But as he came abreast of them, they would dance in circles around him. Even when he ran full tilt, he could not keep ahead. When, out of breath, he slowed down, the shoes would slow down too, but they would not let him pass them.

Soon the woodcutters' huts were left behind, and they were deep among the trees. Here, in the half-light, butterflies fluttered palely above the ferns, and from somewhere deep in the wood, he could hear a woodpecker. A beetle on the path was being attacked by ants. He rescued it. The forest was so quiet that, when a magpie flew across in a clatter of black and white, it startled him for a moment. "One for sorrow, two for joy. . . ." He peered hopefully into the bushes but could not see a second one. Ahead of them, in a flicker of sunlight, some small animal slipped across the path. A weasel, perhaps, or a large-sized vole. The little shoes danced after it into the bracken, and James followed clumsily. He stood waist-high in brambles and bracken, but could see nothing. No movement, except where he himself had stirred the fronds. Then, there were the shoes again, ahead on the sandy track—dancing, dancing. "Little varmints!" the old man had called them. James rather agreed with him, pushing his painful way out of the brambles.

From then on he took no notice if, from time to time, they flew off into the undergrowth after anything that took their fancy; if he kept to the track, they would always appear again eventually, always a little way ahead. He suddenly began to feel, not afraid exactly, but a little lonely. It was the first time, on one of these trips, that he had strayed away from Mildred—with all her nice certainties and sound common sense. These little red varmints might be taking him anywhere. "At least," he comforted himself, "I know the way back."

At last there came a gleam of sunlight ahead: it was his clearing.

He could see the fallen tree with its upturned roots and silvery branches and could hear the first faint mutter of the stream.

The red shoes marked time for a moment, and then—in a lightning flash, almost faster than his eye could follow—they flew at the fallen tree. He followed more slowly, and there, below the place where Mildred had sat writing her notes, he saw, among the dead leaves and the heavy gleam of moss, something that shone and winked, reflecting the light around. It was—he saw as he came closer—another pair of slippers, but these were cloth of gold. One lay on its side as though carelessly thrown down. He recognized them immediately: these were Dulcibel's shoes.

He heard a sound and, raising his eyes, he saw Dulcibel herself. She was running up the slope toward him from the stream. Her golden dress was hitched up to her knees; her feet were bare and muddy; the circlet had slipped sideways on her tangled hair, and as she ran, she sobbed. When she reached him, she clung on to him. Her little snub nose was pink with weeping, and her cheeks were streaked with tears.

"What is it? What's happened, Dulcibel?" he cried, catching her by the arms. The little red shoes danced excitedly about them. She broke away from him and sank to the ground, her face in her hands. She could not speak for sobbing.

He kneeled down beside her. He thought of the magpie and its message: "One for sorrow." "Tell me, Dulcibel! Tell me quickly—"

"You can guess!" gasped Dulcibel, raising her face at last. "It's awful, it's terrible! That link broke again, and now the ball's in the well!"

EIGHT

She calmed down after a while, and James, sitting beside her, found he was holding her hand. "Why didn't you fish it out at once?"

"It sank!" she gasped. "It went down at once, as though someone or something had clutched it! Then the courtyard went dark—like before a storm or as though it were evening. And the water in the well went dark like mud and began to swirl and bubble. Oh, it was awful!" She hid her face again.

"Go on," said James.

"Then a voice said—"

"What sort of voice?"

"A deep sort of hollow voice. Croaky. It said—" She thought for a moment, making sure she got the words right. "Yes, I'll never forget it. It said:

" 'Have thee I will
And here ye'll bide.
There'll be no place
Where thou canst hide.
In seven days
Thou'lt be my bride.' "

"Goodness!" said James. After a moment, he added, "Well, that gives us a week anyway."

"And then," she went on, looking fearful again, "someone or something laughed in the shadows."

"What sort of something?"

"I don't know." She thought for a moment. "But I think I can guess. I wish those shoes would go away."

"They're all right," said James. He pulled up a tuft of grass and studied it thoughtfully. "How did this spell come about in the first place?"

"Oh, the usual way," said Dulcibel. "A bad fairy at the christening."

"Why do they always talk in rhyme?"

"It's the custom," said Dulcibel. Her voice still shuddered a little from her recent sobs.

"What have they got against you?"

"I don't know. You never do know. You see, it would be very embarrassing for my father and mother to have a daughter living down a well and married to a toad. They wouldn't know what to say to people." She wiped her hand across her eyes to smooth the tears away. Then she straightened her little crown. "Bad fairies enjoy that kind of situation. But if I refuse, we all disappear into thin air—the palace, courtiers, gardens, and everything."

"That might be better than living down a well."

"Well, you never know," said Dulcibel, "and it would be my fault. And yet"—she almost smiled—"I can't sort of see my father disappearing into thin air. Or my mother either for that matter."

"Who did you think it was laughing in the shadows?"

"I thought it was Pinprickel. I'm *sure* it was Pinprickel."

"Who's Pinprickel?"

"The bad fairy who came to the christening." She stood up, worried again suddenly. "There's only one thing to do."

"What's that?"

"Find that other toad. The one with a jewel in its head. It's just a chance. If you'd help me . . ."

"Yes, I'll help you," said James, "but it's no good looking in the stream."

"I know that really."

"You said yourself you thought someone had it."

"I still do—really."

"Then we've got to make inquiries. Ask about—without quite seeming to, if you know what I mean. Somebody rather old might know, somebody who remembers things." He thought of the two Jacks. Then another idea struck him. "I know—" He, too, sprang to his feet. "Are you frightened of witches?"

"Yes," said Dulcibel.

"So am I, as a matter of fact. But a witch might be our best chance. We sort of need somebody who knows about magic. That one you spoke of, remember? I think perhaps she may live somewhere quite near. Can you remember her name?"

Dulcibel thought for a moment. "No," she said at last, "I did hear it. But now I can't remember."

"It wouldn't be Hecubenna, by any chance?"

"Hecubenna?" Dulcibel frowned and then her face cleared. "Hecubenna! Yes, that was the name. Yes, I'm sure that was the name. Hecubenna . . ." she repeated.

Then James told her about the bull's horns and the charm and that well-trodden path leading into the bushes. "That's the path we've got to take," he said.

"Oh, please!" said Dulcibel. "I would really rather not."

"Oh, come on, Dulcibel. Be brave. I'm sure it's the right thing to do."

"Oh, *please* not," said Dulcibel.

"Think of living down that well for ever and ever! Think of your parents disappearing into thin air. Oh, come on, Dulcibel. It's worth a try. Look at those shoes—how they're dancing! They're dying to take us."

"I don't like those shoes," said Dulcibel.

"Well, then you're ungrateful," said James. "It was those shoes that brought me to you."

Dulcibel was silent a moment, and then she said sulkily, "I'll come as far as the door."

"Well, come on then," said James. "Put your slippers on. And let down your dress. You look awful like that."

"I can't walk fast with my dress down," complained Dulcibel as the little shoes scampered away.

"You don't have to keep up with them," explained James. "They're only showing off. They soon come back to you if you keep on at your own pace."

As they made their way down the path, with the red shoes dancing ahead, James asked Dulcibel how she had known where to find him.

"They said you were going to Much-Belungun-under-Bluff. And you can see the Bluff from my courtyard. I sort of guessed there was a way through the forest."

"How did you get away from the palace? I mean, it's so heavily guarded—all those halberdiers and things?"

"I ran down through the shrubbery to the postern gate. And" —she turned an amazed face toward him—"I found it unlocked! I don't know what made me go there—it's always kept locked. But there it was—I turned the ring and it opened! It must have been magic."

"No, it wasn't magic. It was Mildred," said James, and he told her about the key.

At last they reached the stricken oak tree, with its shabby, nailed-up charm. "What's that?" asked Dulcibel uneasily. And James explained to her about Big Hans and the evil eye, and how the charm kept it off.

The path beside the tree wound away between nettles and brambles into the shadows of the trees. The little red shoes darted into it. It was well worn but rather muddy.

"You can see," said James, "that somebody uses it. I think she must still be there."

"I don't think I want to go any farther . . ." faltered Dulcibel. She eyed the path with distaste.

"Oh, come on, Dulcibel. Come a little way. It might take hours. You don't want to stay here alone."

"No, I don't," admitted Dulcibel unhappily. "All right, I'll come a little way."

The path, as it wound into the trees, became darker and more sunless with every step they took. Dulcibel squealed when something slithered past her foot and said it was a snake.

"I didn't see anything," said James. But he took a firmer grip on his thumb stick.

"It *was* a snake. I know it was! Oh, please, let us go back!"

"Please, Dulcibel, try to be brave. Look, it's getting lighter ahead."

Dulcibel raised her eyes. Yes, it was getting lighter, and the trees seemed to be thinning. She pressed her lips together in a dogged kind of way and, lifting her skirt from the mud, plodded again on after James. The little red shoes were hurrying on ahead, and they could hear the sound of singing. And then, at last, they saw the cottage.

It wasn't at all like a witch's cottage—at least, like none they had imagined: neatly thatched and freshly whitewashed. There was a little garden with wattle fencing, filled with flowers and many kinds of vegetables. A line of washing stirred gently in the sunshine, slung between two cherry trees. As they came closer, the singing stopped abruptly and a voice said, "Mercy to goodness!"

A rosy woman, her skirt turned up over her petticoats, had taken a clothespin out of her mouth and was staring at them curiously. She seemed very much surprised. Who could they be, her expression seemed to say, this girl in a golden dress and this boy in a jacket, whose red pantaloons were not even cross-gartered?

"Good day to you," said James, in the manner of Mildred.

"Good day, little master," said the woman uncertainly.

"Good day," said Dulcibel.

"I think," said James, "we may have come to the wrong place. We were looking"—he hesitated shyly—"we were looking for someone called Hecubenna."

The woman's face lit up. "Oh, you mean Auntie?" she smiled at them now in a friendly kind of way as such women do with children. Then, as if sorry to disappoint them, she went on: "She's past it now, you know. People don't come here any more."

"Oh," said James, nonplussed. He thought for a moment and then he said, "Why not?"

"She's retired like." (But everybody knew that: where could they have come from, these children?) "But she likes a bit of a visitor now and again. You wait there a moment, and I'll see what she says. . . ."

When she had gone away into the cottage, Dulcibel said, "I'm going to stay out here." There was a rustic seat near the porch, and she sat down on it. She still looked very nervous.

As the woman emerged again on the threshold, there was a scuffle in the doorway. "Out! Out!" she cried, flapping her apron. "I won't have you in here. Out you go, I say!" The little red shoes came scuffling down the path and disappeared into the cabbages. "Did you bring them?" she asked James as she came up to him.

"Well, they brought us really," said James.

"A real nuisance, those shoes are getting," said the woman. "I can't think what's come over them lately." She smiled at the children. "Come you in," she said. "She'd like to see ye." They noticed she had let down her skirt and had put on a clean white apron. "Now don't you excite her, mind. One at a time is best."

"I'll come in," said James. Dulcibel looked relieved.

It seemed rather dark inside by reason of the small, deep-set windows, but the little room was spotless. Two black cats rose lazily from a rag rug before the hearth. They stretched themselves, yawned, and went out into the sunlight. "They'll be after those shoes in a minute," said the woman, "you'll see if they don't. Not that they ever catch them."

James was staring past her at a figure by the fire: a very ancient figure, wrapped in a dark shawl, seated in a large wooden chair. The eyes in the shriveled face were very dark and bright. She had just the hooked nose that James imagined she would have, and some white hairs on her chin. In one shaking hand she held a wooden spoon. There was a bowl upon her knee.

"See what I've brought you, Auntie!" said the woman, bending over her and raising her voice. "A nice boy come to see you."

The old woman stared at James for a moment. Her jaws were working slowly, and her bright, dark eyes seemed to glisten. "That's a fine boy," she croaked at last. "I could eat a fine, plump boy like that!"

The younger woman laughed. "You could have, Auntie, but you're past it now."

"What's that you say?"

"I said you could have"—she raised her voice even higher—"but your teeth is past it now."

The old woman began to laugh. Her shoulders shook with merriment. She gazed across at James, her black eyes twinkling between their reddened lids. "I han't got no teeth," she said, and went on laughing as though this were a great joke. There was such mischief in the old face that James smiled too.

The younger woman turned to James. "Sit ye down," she said in her normal voice. "You don't want to take notice of what she says: she does it apurpose to see how folks'll act. She ain't eaten a child yet. She'd boil up things in that great pot yonder"—she pointed to the hearth—"all sorts of rubbish—things you wouldn't like to name. But she was always one for rabbit herself—wild conies, we call 'em—or a nice roast fowl." She raised her voice again. "Now, you eat up your porridge, Auntie, and then we'll see. . . ." See what? wondered James.

"Not that she hasn't done marvels in her time. Wonderful, you might say she's been. People coming from far and wide—I can't tell you! As for spells, there's never been one like her! Put spells about like a flock of starlings, as you might say, on high and low, castle and cottage—and most of them still working."

"I know," said James, remembering Pinprickel.

"She had others working for her then. She gave them their orders like, and off they'd go. Twenty-seven bad fairies she had at one time, sending 'em off here, there, and everywhere. Not to mention the betwixt and betweens—like Rumpelstiltskin."

"Oh," said James, his memory stirring faintly, "was he one of hers?"

"Well, yes, until he got too independent like. There was a bit of a rumpus, and she soon sent him packing." She was silent a moment, as though thinking this over. "He never did so well on his own. Oh yes," she went on, "Auntie's had her day all right. She's done real wonders in her time. But now she's past it." She glanced across at the old crone who, still chuckling to herself, was wielding her shaky spoon: there was pride in the younger woman's glance and true affection. "They don't come like her any more."

"Could she fly?" asked James after a moment.

"Fly! She'd be up that bluff like a leaf on the wind. Once a month regular, at full moon. There was a herb she needed which only grew at that height. Oh yes, she could fly all right."

James was silent a moment, suitably impressed. After a while he asked, "Could she take a spell off?"

"Not now she couldn't." She sighed. "And it wouldn't be fair to ask her." She turned to James, suddenly curious. "Had you anything in mind?"

"Yes, I had in a way," said James. He looked back at the pleasant,

rosy face. She reminded him of someone, but he could not remember who. Should he tell her everything, perhaps, and ask her advice?

She was looking at him quietly, and then she said, "Where do you hail from, child?"

James thought for a moment. "Much-Belungun-under-Bluff," he said at last.

"That's my village," she told him. "Where would ye be biding?"

"At the inn. I don't know its name."

"With the two Jacks?"

"That's right."

"They could never agree what to call it: one wanted to name it 'At the sign of the Beanstalk,' the other 'The Giant's Head.' But they're two good fellers, and that's a fact. Ye couldn't be in better hands. My mam takes care of them, like I do"—she nodded toward the old woman—"of her." So this, thought James, was why this cheerful face looked so familiar; she was "the widder-woman's" daughter. "After I lost my man, I took her in hand like. . . ." Again she nodded toward the ancient crone. "The place was a pigsty, nay worse; the thatch all gone and she with a fortune in gold and silver pieces hid behind the chimney breast. But she was good to me when my John was taken bad—potions and such like. But her best days were gone and over, though I didn't see it at the time. What do they call you, child?" James told her. She smiled and repeated his name and then she said, "They call me 'Mistress Tab.' 'Tabitha' they christened me. My mother's called Dame Wellbeloved."

James was beginning to realize that, if it was information he wanted, he had come to the right place. Perhaps because of her lonely life, Mistress Tabitha seemed happy to keep him by her and willing to tell him much.

"What about that little girl? Won't she come inside?"

James hesitated. "She's all right," he said. "She—she likes the sunshine."

"She's a princess, isn't she?"

"Yes," said James.

"Which princess?" asked Mistress Tab.

James decided to tell her everything: it was the only way, he realized, that they might get help. "Princess Dulcibel," he said.

She recognized the name at once. She knew the whole story—Boofy and Belle and Beau, Pumpkin, who had been Cinderella, the well, and the dreaded toad. "Not that I've been over that way myself," she said. "I mean"—and she laughed—"who would ask the likes of me to a palace? But I've heard it's a lovely place they've got there. Except—" and her face clouded. James told her then what had happened: the darkness, the voice, the swirling water, and the terrible fate facing Dulcibel.

"So it's happened at last!" she exclaimed, and sat for a moment in silence, looking very unhappy. The old woman in her chair by the fireside had stopped eating and was watching them closely.

James asked then about the other toad, the one with a jewel in its head. "We thought you might have it here," he said.

The woman shook her head sadly. She sighed. She turned her clear gaze toward the witch by the fire and sighed again. "It was here," she said. "Auntie had it and for many a long year. But 'tis here no longer. It was more a frog than a toad," she went on, "a lovely pale green, they say it was. But she lost it. Before my time, that was. After she lost that frog, she began to lose her powers."

"How did she lose it?" asked James, hardly aware as yet of his deep disappointment.

"She always took it with her when she went up the Bluff. Because of the giant. She was safe with her frog, you see. She'd carry it with her in the bottom of a basket, the basket she took for herbs. One day, she set the basket on the ground and, maybe, it fell on its side. As she ran to set it to rights, a great shadow fell across her. It was the giant. She took fright and thrust the herbs into the basket and ran to the edge of the Bluff and was off into space like a gannet. . . ."

"What was she riding?" asked James, thinking of broomsticks.

"I don't know what she was riding," replied Tabitha, in a sad, colorless voice, "but it was only when she got home and unpacked the herbs that she saw the frog had gone." She was silent a moment and then she said, "Nothing would go right after that. That giant has got it still, I wouldn't wonder."

"Has got it," repeated James. "You mean—he's still alive?"

"Of course he's alive," said Mistress Tab, "so long as he's got that frog." She spoke in a tone of great weariness. "Doesn't seem fair to Auntie. . . ."

"But," said James, "there were thirteen giants—that's what I've heard—and the Giant-Killer killed them all."

"He killed twelve," said Tabitha, in the same spiritless voice. "That's his trouble. That's what worries him. And Jack-of-the-Beanstalk—he never knows how he grew that plant: it sprang up all in one night, you remember? He can't do it again. They think they're past it. It worries them."

James thought of Dulcibel. He thought of Boofy and Beau and Belle and Pumpkin, disappearing into thin air. He thought of the toad (or was it a frog?) in the well. "Isn't there any way up the Bluff?" he said.

Tabitha got up from the window seat and crossed the room to the fireplace. She leaned over the old woman. "Is there any way up the Bluff, Auntie," she shouted, "bar flying?"

The old woman thought for a moment.

"Well, there's the crevice . . ." she said unwillingly, and slightly shook her head.

NINE

As they walked back through the winding path, James told Dulcibel all he had found out. Before leaving, the woman had given them a bowl of milk each, which they drank on the bench in the sunshine, and a little linen bag filled with gingerbread and cherries for refreshment on their way. She had been very kind and more than a little worried. The red shoes had disappeared: perhaps their job was done? They made their way back to the clearing, although it was not on their way back to the village. But it was pleasant to sit on the fallen tree and eat their gingerbread and to listen to the sound of the stream. It was a good, quiet place in which to think and talk. Not that Dulcibel said much: she had become desperately and unhappily silent.

"Everybody in this kingdom seems to have retired," said James, "except you," he added. After a moment he threw away his last cherry pit, and stood up. "Come on," he said.

"Where can we go?" asked Dulcibel unhappily.

"We better go back to Much-Belungun." He took her by the elbow and urged her to her feet. "We might find Mildred there."

"What can *she* do?" asked Dulcibel.

"You never know," said James.

But when they reached Much-Belungun, the village seemed as empty as before. The door of the inn was closed (against the little shoes, no doubt). James pulled on the string of the latch, and they went inside. There sat the two old men, one on each side of the fire, staring into it: very dejected they looked. But, seeing James, they both jumped up and came toward him, smiling with relief. They had been very worried, he realized.

"Couldn't think where you could've got to," said Jack-of-the-Beanstalk.

"Nor what to tell Mildred, like, if you didn't come back," said the other. They both stared at Dulcibel. "What's this you've brought? A fairy?"

"No, it's a princess," said James and introduced them.

They made her welcome and drew her to the table, and Big Jack got busy at the fire. The table, James saw, was set for a meal. "But we hadn't the heart to eat," explained Jack-the-Giant-Killer.

Jack-of-the-Beanstalk stood smiling happily at Dulcibel. "Haven't had a princess, not in Much-Belungun, not in this place, for many a long year," he said proudly. "Wait till all those silly folk get back from the wedding. They'll be surprised, and no mistake. Wager some of them'd never got close enough to see the bridesmaids, let alone the bride and groom!"

At this point Dulcibel bowed her head over the table and burst into tears.

"She's in terrible trouble," said James.

The old men were very distressed. Jack-of-the-Beanstalk found a little pewter mug and plied her with cordial, so strong and spicy that she spluttered at the first sip. The Giant-Killer set a bowl of hot soup before her, begging her to "sup a drop." She smiled at them through her tears: no longer a princess to them but "a poor little maid." They put off asking questions until a little had been eaten and drunk. It was very little. And then they found a cushion for her and put her on a stool by the fire. Then they filled their pipes and waited.

It was James who told them what had happened, with small interruptions from Dulcibel as gradually she became calmer. When the old men heard that the ball had fallen into the well, they shook their heads gravely: they knew what this meant. Jack-the-Giant-Killer only became excited when they described their meeting with the witch. He got up from his stool and stumped about on the flagstones; he made fists of his hands and raised them in the air. "There's no giant living on the Bluff," he kept saying, "there's no giant living!"

"He always says that," explained Jack-of-the-Beanstalk. He stooped over the fire to knock his pipe out, and turning his head to James, he added in a low voice, "But there is, you know."

When James, explaining what Tabitha had told him, got to the bit about the frog, Jack-the-Giant-Killer stopped his pacing and came toward them eagerly. "What's that you say? What's that?" he almost shouted, taking James by the arm. James explained again. "It's a talisman," he said.

"Magic," said Dulcibel.

The Giant-Killer straightened up. He was thinking deeply and staring into the distance. By the fire, the others waited in silence. At last the Giant-Killer gave a great sigh. "So that explains it," he said, in a voice that was almost normal, "that explains *why*—try as I might—I never was able to get him!"

There was a short, shocked silence in the room and then a sense of relief: he had admitted the truth at last. Jack-of-the-Beanstalk came over toward his friend and laid a kindly hand on his arm. "So you see, now, Jack, it wasn't your lack of skill."

"No," repeated the Giant-Killer, "it wasn't my lack of skill." He spoke quietly, with a kind of wonder in his voice. "A talisman," he repeated. "I never thought of that. . . ."

"So long as he had that frog, no one could have got him. However strong, however brave—" Jack-of-the-Beanstalk, still patting the arm of his friend, turned back to James. "You see," he explained, "there was a time when the giants of the Bluff could get down into the valley. Some sort of rocky track they knew of—back there between the mountains. One at a time they'd come, as the fancy took them. But one was enough, believe you me: he'd take our cattle, kidnap our maidens, tread down our young men, and I can't say what else. No use hiding in the forest—why, they'd pull up the trees by the roots and kick down our houses and barns. They'd take our grain, in great sacks, with the maidens and cattle mixed up with the barley and oats. Some years, maybe three on end, not a giant would come: that track of theirs was dangerous—great boulders all ready to topple and waterfalls in between. But come they did, all the same. Now, Jack here, studied their ways. There were thirteen giants in all, and he got to know 'em, one by one. And, one by one, he picked them off. He took his time. Well, you know his stories. . . . Some he'd pick off one way, some another. Until none but one remained. But this one would come down, every few months or so, and there'd be havoc in the land. But could Jack get him? Couldn't even set eyes on him—except once in the distance like—but there was the damage done. A charmed life that giant seemed to have. You know what Jack did?"

"No," breathed James.

"He took a keg of gunpowder and blew up the giants' pass!"

"Goodness!" said James.

"And after that we had peace." There was a short silence. Jack-of-the-Beanstalk took a few quick pulls on his pipe: his listeners felt there was something more to come.

Jack-the-Giant-Killer sat down suddenly beside the table. He put his head in his hands. After a moment he looked up again. " 'Twas many a long weary mile to that pass. But I followed his tracks, like—hefty great tracks giants leave."

"Then he came home again," went on Jack-of-the-Beanstalk, "and made his plans, taking his time, as usual. And 'twas an earthquake he made. You could hear it here in Much-Belungun. As I said, after that there was peace. Real peace, at last. Jack could not help but think he had blown up the giant, too."

"It stood to reason," said Jack-the-Giant-Killer.

"*Until*," went on Jack-of-the-Beanstalk, in a slow, mysterious voice, "the muck began to come down. . . ."

"What muck?" asked Dulcibel, looking rather pale.

"That muck at the foot of the Bluff. Threw all his rubbish down: skins, bones, rotting greenstuff, everything you could think of. The flies in summer were something chronic. Did it to spite us, I shouldn't wonder. And to show he was still alive."

Jack-the-Giant-Killer looked up. "There hasn't been so much, not lately," he said.

"That doesn't prove anything," said Jack-of-the-Beanstalk.

"You see," went on Jack-the-Giant-Killer in the same rather colorless voice, "when I set up that horse's tail, I thought he was finished and gone. It was to make up the numbers, like." He seemed to have become depressed again.

"But still he worries," went on Jack-of-the-Beanstalk. "Look at him, now. Shamed he's always been that he didn't get that last one. We gave out, of course, that *all* the giants were dead. Once their track was gone and we felt safe, like. And people believed us, until they saw the muck. 'Twas the sight of that muck got Jack down. Very down, he got."

"You got down yourself," said the Giant-Killer wearily, "planting all those beans, and nothing much coming up. You see," he explained to James, "we thought if he could get a beanstalk to grow, like the one that came up in the night—I might go up it, armed with my sling and my crossbow, but, somehow, he'd lost the knack."

James, too, began to feel rather down: there seemed to be nothing anyone could do—Dulcibel, poor frightened Dulcibel, must go to her fate. There was a longish silence, and then he said timidly, "Did you try the crevice?"

"Try the crevice! Of course I tried the crevice! I were young and strong then—there was nothing I wouldn't try. Seems all right at first, that crevice, but it narrows down to nothing—two faces of solid rock: you couldn't get a knife blade between 'em. And you couldn't use gunpowder: that whole Bluff would come down."

There was another silence. Then Dulcibel said in her clear treble, "And even if you *had* got up, he'd have had his frog to keep him safe."

"That's right," said Jack-of-the-Beanstalk glumly.

"That's right," agreed the Giant-Killer. He sighed.

Once again they all four sat without speaking. James was thinking furiously. After a while, he said shyly, "Would it be a trouble to you if—if Dulcibel stayed here until Mildred gets back?"

"Trouble? 'Twould be an honor." Jack-the-Giant-Killer rose from the table. "Poor little maiden. . . ."

"She can bide in the white room under the rafters. Gets the full sun," said Jack-of-the-Beanstalk. (This was the room, James found out later, that the old men kept for Mildred.)

Jack-the-Giant-Killer, on his way to the door, paused in his tracks. Turning slightly, he stared at the far wall: he was thinking deeply. After a moment he crossed the room and unhooked a tress from the wall. It was the thirteenth tress. He stared down at it as it hung from his hand and sorrowfully shook his head. They watched him anxiously as he came back to the hearth and deliberately moved two pots: then, just as deliberately, he drew back his arm and flung the tress on the fire. It blazed up immediately, lighting their startled faces, and making an awful smell. Jack watched it thoughtfully, dusting his hands together, and then he turned away. "Well, that's that," he said, smiling around at them. It was a very wan little smile.

TEN

They went to bed early. They were very tired. Dame Wellbeloved, "the widder-woman," gave Dulcibel a little shift to sleep in. It had belonged to her granddaughter, who long since had grown out of it. She took away the mud-stained golden dress to make it "better than new." James woke once, when a door banged and he heard a scraping sound on the flagged floor next door. Opening a sleepy eye, he saw it was still dusk. Then the silence in the house, the utter silence, told him that the old men had gone out. He slept again. And slept and slept.

In the morning, it was "the widder-woman" who gave them their breakfast. The old men had long since eaten and were now about their business. Dame Wellbeloved had produced for Dulcibel (from the same source as the little shift) a gray frieze skirt, a red flannel petticoat, and a little velvet bodice laced with ribbon.

"You look like a goose girl," James told Dulcibel at breakfast. But Dulcibel did not mind: she felt comfortable in these clothes—cloth of gold could sometimes be a little scratchy.

There seemed nothing to do. They sat on the window seat and stared out through the geraniums. The Green was deserted. The day was overcast.

"I wish Mildred would come," James would say at intervals, and Dulcibel would reply, "But what could she *do*?"

"One thing," said James, after a brief wander around the room, "they'd never think of looking for you here."

"You don't know Pinprickel," said Dulcibel.

James looked at the place on the far wall where the thirteenth tress had hung. It was whiter than the grayish lime-washed space around it. Everything was turning out very sad, very difficult, very dangerous. He glanced up at the bean case: it was empty. This, too? Why had the bean been removed? Was it through kindness and delicacy from one Jack to the other—"You've burnt your tress, I'll burn my bean"? Both admitting some kind of failure? But, thought James, such thoughtfulness seemed a little farfetched: the bean, at any rate, had been real.

"Would you like to go for a walk?" he asked Dulcibel later in the morning. "Would you like to take a look at that crevice?"

"It's full of bats and hobgoblins," said Dulcibel. "I don't mind hobgoblins, but I hate bats. Look, they're coming back from the wedding."

James went to the window. Several carts were arriving, dusty and luggage-laden. Tired mothers, at various doorways, lifted down sleeping children. Red-faced, grumbling men hauled on packages and rubbed their weary eyes. Some lifted their voices in anger, some slunk indoors. Listless boys led away the mules and horses. Cottage doors shut, and again the Green was silent.

"I wish Mildred would come," said James.

Dulcibel, staring out of the window, said, "Here comes another lot. They'll be arriving all day now. And all day tomorrow, too, I wouldn't wonder." She sighed tremulously, "Some princesses are lucky; they don't have to marry toads."

James was silent. There seemed to be nothing to say. He wanted to take her hand; he wanted to comfort her, but what was the good? "Let's go out," he said.

But as Dulcibel felt with her toes under the window seat for her kicked-off golden shoes, Dame Wellbeloved bustled in to lay the table.

"We were just going for a little stroll," James explained uncertainly.

"What! With a fat capon on the back spit!" exclaimed Dame Wellbeloved (and certainly a delicious aroma had followed her in at the door). "And spiced pig's head in jelly, made specially by *him*. . . ." She panted a little as she set the table. "And the other one, coming up the path now, with fresh cresses, radishes, and the Lord knows what else. . . ."

So they stayed and ate with the kind old men, plied with strange drinks and strange, delicious foods–so carefully thought out and prepared for them. After eating, the old men seemed tired: in such quiet lives, Mildred and her "guests" perhaps had been a little too much for them? James saw one old man nod, then wake himself quickly by raising his head. The other closed his eyes for a moment, as though deep in thought, but opened them swiftly at the scrape of a chair and pressed Dulcibel to take a sugar plum. Cross as they might be sometimes with each other, toward the children their courtesy did not falter.

But there was a sense of misery in the air, an uncertainty that felt like dread. The children withdrew again to the window seat when the old men settled themselves by the fire. Soon they heard some heavy breathing and the soft, whistling sound of a snore. "Let's go out," whispered James.

They crept to the door and silently lifted the latch and, once outside, closed it with equal care. People were still arriving in various kinds of vehicles–very tired, they all seemed and very dusty. They barely glanced up as James and Dulcibel wended their way through the village–a boy in a leather jacket and a girl in a frieze skirt. Strangers, no doubt, but nobody seemed to care.

Soon they were under the Bluff, but where was the crevice?

"Let's try this way," said James and went on ahead to where the Bluff seemed to turn around a corner. Once past this curve in the face of the cliff, they could no longer see the village. Some way ahead of them, at the base of the rock, they could see a fall of boulders. "It'll be there," said James.

And it was. A boulder-strewn cavern, it seemed like at first, but staring in, they could see it went back and back, narrowing unevenly between ledges and faces of rock. It was a gash in the overhanging Bluff, as though cut by some great crooked knife into a tough and crumbly cake.

"Let's go in," said James.

"But the *bats*!" exclaimed Dulcibel.

The bats will all be asleep now—it's still daylight," said James. He looked up into the ledges and crevices above. "Look, you can see them—hanging in bunches. They won't hurt you," he assured her.

Gingerly, she followed him in, picking her way from boulder to boulder. "They might get into my hair," she complained.

"That's an old wives' tale," James called back to her from the half-light and shadows ahead. And from somewhere above them came the echo, ". . . ives tale . . . ives tale. . . ."

James, always a keen rock-climber, as he went in deeper, was climbing up and up. He could not resist it while the footholds were good.

"Where are you going?" wailed Dulcibel, and the echo answered, ". . . owing . . . owing. . . ."

"Just to see," said James. "Come on. It's all right."

She followed him, rather than be alone with the bats. It was a steady ascent up the inside heart of the crevice, not too difficult but naturally somewhat tiring. Feeling for footholds, pulling on ledges took all their attention and breath. A faint light seemed to come from somewhere other than that which seeped in through the entrance below.

James was enjoying himself: he felt confident and light. On a sudden ledge, stretching back behind him into darkness, he sat and rested, waiting for Dulcibel. His eyes had become used to the dimness, and he had time to look around him: there was a series of ledges and crannies and shelf-like receding caverns. As he sat on the rock edge, his legs hanging down, the stone beneath his hands felt worn and smooth: it had a used feeling. Suddenly he heard a scraping sound, followed by a dry slither. Was it Dulcibel? No, he could hear her panting up the rocks below. This sound came from in front of him, just across the narrow chasm: something was moving slowly, almost painfully, toward the edge of the opposite rock. Then he saw it, a snoutlike face, dully glowing eyes, a scaly body, some kind of wings with claw-like talons attached. It was the talons that scraped and the body that slithered. It came to the edge of the rock and stared at him. Just stared—but James did not like it at all. Then, to his dismay, he heard other scrapings, other slitherings. They seemed all around him. Painfully moving creatures emerging slowly from all the hollows and crannies. They looked very much alike, some smaller, some larger; their glowing eyes faintly lit the rocks and crags around as the lamps of miners light a coal face. They did not attempt to touch him. At a respectful distance, they became still—just staring.

He gripped the rock edge with his hands, nor daring to move or speak. It was with great relief he heard Dulcibel approaching. At last her flushed face appeared at the level of his knees; two more steps and she swung herself up beside him on the ledge.

"Phew! That was a climb!" she said, fanning her face with her hand. James was amazed—could she not see these dreadful creatures that surrounded them? But she had seen them: she stretched out a friendly hand and patted one of them on the head. "Hobgoblins," she said. Hobgoblins—so this is what they were like! "They're very helpless, except on the wing," Dulcibel went on, "and they mate for life," she added. James looked more closely at those dreadful, snoutish faces—the large, sad, shining eyes below the knobby brows.

"Oh, look!" said Dulcibel in a delighted voice. "One's brought its baby!" And there, under a leathery wing, James saw the snoutish face in miniature; a little fearful, it looked, as though James might try to grab it.

"I didn't think goblins looked like that," said James.

"They don't," said Dulcibel. "These are hobgoblins."

"They're rather like those things," said James, eyeing the strange bodies, "which stick out on the roofs of old churches." He put out a tentative hand and laid it on the knobbly head that was nearest. He stroked the head, and the heavy lidded eyes closed slowly and then gently opened.

"They loved being stroked," said Dulcibel. After a while she said, "Shall we go back now?"

James looked upward into the receding crevice: there were still some very good footholds. "I'd rather like to go up a bit farther," he said. When Dulcibel did not reply immediately, he went on, "You could wait here if you like."

Dulcibel thought for a moment and then she said, "No, I'll come with you."

So on they went again. James, going first, often turned to lend a hand to Dulcibel. But she needed it less and less often: she was really quite good at climbing. Perhaps, thought James, it was all those staircases in the palace that had kept her muscles in trim. Suddenly, having turned a corner, they saw above them a narrow gleam of light, which lit up their faces as they gazed upward. It was almost a slice of light.

"This is it," said James.

"What do you mean?" asked Dulcibel.

James stared thoughtfully upward. "The place where the two rock faces nearly meet. It was a bit of an exaggeration to say you couldn't get a knife between them." He thought again for a moment. "You *could*, you know."

"Yes," said Dulcibel, "but not a person."

"Not a person, not a great, big-shouldered person like Jack-the-Giant-Killer must have been. But"—he narrowed his eyes in calculation while the light struck downwards on his face—"but a *child* might squeeze through sideways. I'm going to try it."

"Oh, please don't!" cried Dulcibel. "You'll only get stuck."

"It's worth a try." He turned around toward her and sat down on the edge of a boulder so, with Dulcibel standing, their eyes were on a level. "Listen, Dulcibel," he said, "have you thought, have you actually realized, that that frog you need might be up there?"

"Yes, of course I have," said Dulcibel. "But so is the giant."

"We're not going to *look* for the frog or the giant or anything like that. At least not today we aren't. All we're going to try to do today is to find out if there is a way up the Bluff—then we can come down again. Don't you understand?"

"Yes," said Dulcibel.

"And don't you think it's worth a try?" He waited a moment. "Say yes, Dulcibel, because you've got to help me."

"All right," said Dulcibel, after some hesitation. "What must I do?"

"I'll show you," said James.

He climbed on ahead, until he stood directly under the crack: it had been formed, he guessed, by one slatey rock that had split itself in half. He stood on a heap of rubble washed through, he supposed, by the rain. Stretching up, he ran his hands over both surfaces of rock. There were slight unevennesses but not many. Dulcibel, who had followed him, stood beside him, quietly waiting.

"Now," he said, "if you'll stand where I am, Dulcibel, and crouch down, I'll put my feet on your shoulders. Do you think you can hold me?"

"I'll try," said Dulcibel. He stood aside from her, and she crouched down obediently in a "knees bend" position.

"That's it," said James. "Keep as straight as you can. . . . Steady yourself on that rock in front of you." When she felt the weight of his soft moccasins against her neck muscles, Dulcibel did sink down a little, but by leaning slightly forward and grasping an outcrop of rock, she found her balance again. "Now stand up very slowly," said James. His hands once again were exploring the walls of the crack. "If I can get my head through," she heard him saying in a muffled voice, "I think the rest of me will follow. . . . Just go on rising up, Dulcibel . . . slowly as you can. . . ." Straining every muscle, she did as she was told, and suddenly the weight lightened as though James were falling forward. "I'm through!" he shouted. The weight had gone from her shoulders, and she could hear the scuffle of James's shoes and a good deal of panting. She leaned against the outcrop of rock in front of her, trying to get her breath. It was very dark suddenly: James was blocking out the light. Then the light came back again, and she could see James's face looking down at her: he seemed to be lying somehow upside down and sideways. "It opens to the side," he told her, his voice very excited. "Give me your hands, Dulcibel. . . . I'll pull you up!"

Dulcibel, exhausted, had sat down on the rubble. "Just a minute . . ." she faltered. James understood. "All right—have a rest. But it's quite easy—you're smaller than me. The crack, once you've got your head through, sort of opens up."

All Dulcibel said was, "Could we get down again?"

"Of course we could: getting down, we'd have gravity to help us."

This did not mean very much to Dulcibel, but she took his word for it. "Give me your hands," said James, "and sort of scramble with your feet . . . that's right . . . now lean over; you've got to come in kind of sideways."

At last she was through, tumbling beside James on a base of stones and rubble. She felt grazed and bruised, and James, who did not seem to notice it, had a red bump over his eye. The deep-sided track now in front of them seemed more like the bed of a stream;

the going was steep but easy, and at last they were in daylight. Above their heads some small clouds scurried across a blue sky. As they climbed, the banks of the gorge became lower. Here and there were clusters of ferns. "We're nearly there," said James.

The last bit became difficult again. Overhung with boulders, which leaned in toward each other, it felt rather like the bottom of a well. Only here and there could they see the sky. James studied the formation of the rocks, and after a while he said to Dulcibel, "I think I see where to go. Just put your hands and feet where I do."

It was not such a difficult climb after all, and they emerged between two leaning rocks into bright afternoon sunlight. They found themselves on the smooth top of a very large boulder, from which they could see all around.

ELEVEN

It was a strange scene, not desolate exactly. The land in front of them rose almost imperceptibly toward the mountains in the background. On it were grazing quite large herds of cattle and sheep. The ground was close-shorn like downland grass, with many outcrops of rock and small stunted bushes. It was strewn with bones, whitened by wind and weather. Against the crags that marked the beginning of the mountains, they saw the castle. It reared up against the rocks and looked like part of them, built as it was of the same stone and partially ruined.

"That's where he lives," said James. Dulcibel shivered and drew closer to him. "If we sit here quietly," James went on, "we might see him."

"He might see us," said Dulcibel.

"That wouldn't matter," said James. "We'd be back down the crevice before he could say Jack Robinson."

"Or Fee-fi-fo-fum," said Dulcibel. "That's more what they're supposed to say."

The sun was getting low in the sky, and the whole scene was lit by a rich and vivid light, almost too vivid to seem real. This, James realized, was because, behind the small scudding clouds, a darker mass was building up over the mountains: the deep slate color threw the foreground into bright relief. The cattle cropped on peacefully. There was no sound except, from somewhat not far away, a faint gurgle of water.

"I suppose that's his larder," said Dulcibel, staring at the cattle. James stood up, his hair blowing in the wind.

"If you look behind you," he said, "you can see the palace." Dulcibel stood up, too.

Yes, there, far below them, was the forest—darkening in the half-light—and far beyond this, on its hill, they could just make out the palace (very small it looked from here) catching the last rays of the sun.

"I wonder what they are all doing," said Dulcibel.

"Worrying about you," said James.

From where they stood they could not see Much-Belungun. It was too close under the Bluff. James turned back. The ruined castle stood out more clearly now against the darkening sky. "I don't believe he's in there," he said at last. "There'd be smoke or something. I say, just look at those cattle!"

Dulcibel swung around quickly, and James heard her give a gasp. The cattle were beginning to run like mad things, passing and repassing each other and turning every which way.

"Warble fly," said James, after a moment.

Dulcibel had become very pale. "But the sheep are doing it, too. It isn't warble fly—it's Pinprickel! She's here! Oh, something awful is going to happen!" She hid her face in her hands.

"How do you know it's Pinprickel?"

"Animals always go on like that when she's about. It's Pinprickel, I tell you!"

The dark mass of cloud had now obscured the setting sun. It poured over the sky like a tide, and with it came the rain. There was a lightning flash and the distant growl of thunder. The cattle, now herding together, were galloping off toward the mountains.

"Quickly!" cried Dulcibel. "Let's get down into the crevice!"

They slid awkwardly down between the boulders into the well-like cavity beneath them. Here, they were sheltered from the rain, though water ran between the stones beneath their feet. And they had not realized how dark it would be, and getting darker every minute. James thought of some very tricky footholds encountered on the climb up: how could he deal with these on a climb down in the dark? It would be better, for the time being, to stay where they were—not quite where they were, with the water running so freely between the stones—it would be better to climb back among the boulders and lie hidden until morning. He explained this to Dulcibel.

"What—stay all night here!" she had exclaimed, and then a swirling rush of water caught her about the ankles: she staggered and nearly fell.

"You see what I mean," said James.

So they climbed back into a hollow between the boulders where the rock face, though uneven and knobbly, felt dry: there was just room to lie down. They could hear the rain beating down in torrents upon the rocks above them, and the gurgle of the water flowing past below.

"There must be a spring among these rocks somewhere," said James, "and it's begun to overflow."

"*Begun* to overflow!" exclaimed Dulcibel. Then, after a while, she added, "Do you think we'll be drowned?"

"Of course not. We can always climb out onto the top of the boulder. Listen!"

Somewhere far down below them, there was an ominous rumble, the clash and clatter of falling stones, then quiet again except for the increasing noise of the water. "This is what *made* this crevice—water, in storms like this." For some reason he spoke in a whisper: Dulcibel's ear was so close—her head was lying on his arm. They spoke very little after that, and as time went by, Dulcibel fell asleep. In a short while, lulled by the heavy mutter of the rain, James too drifted off. After all the excitement and the long, hard climb, both were very tired.

TWELVE

When they awoke, it was early dawn. Both felt very cramped and stiff. They could hear many drippings but no sound of running water. It took a little time to remember what had happened and where they were. Before starting on the climb down, they decided to take one more look at this strange land above the Bluff and wait for the light to strengthen. So they clambered out once more onto the top of the boulder. The sun was rising over the mountains; the grass, the rocks, the shrubs (even the bones) looked glistening and peaceful. There was no sign of the cattle. Dulcibel was shivering a little, but as the sun's golden warmth crept out toward them, she seemed to revive.

"Look!" she said suddenly: she was staring at the castle. A curl of smoke was eddying above the roof. As they watched, it thickened and billowed more heavily. "He's alive! He's there!" cried Dulcibel in a panic. She rose to her feet. "Let's go down . . . quickly, quickly!"

James rose more slowly. "I'd like to have seen him just once," he said.

"No, no!" cried Dulcibel. "He's awful . . . he's terrible! I know all about giants—they can always catch you: they can cover the ground so quickly with their great, enormous legs. That smoke means he's got his pot on, and he'd pop us into it, clothes and all, with whatever else is there. They're not particular."

They clambered down again into the crevice and, picking their way over wet stones and rock pools, began their careful descent. In some places the walls of the crevice had fallen in, and they had to climb over quite large rocks. A fear was growing in James's mind: a fear, which for Dulcibel's sake, he dare not express. She was being so eager, so agile, so almost happy in the thought of getting away. They came to the steep places, where they had to cling and slide and feel for footholds, and then at last to the passage that led to the crack. It was as James had feared—a great boulder had fallen across it, from the side, and piled against the boulder a tumble of stones brought down by the torrent in the night. Here was the final pileup, halted by the "knife-blade" creek. It was a pileup weighing many, many tons.

Silent and stunned, they could hardly take it in. Were they to spend the rest of their lives in this crevice because outside it, on the pastures above, there dwelt a giant?

Dulcibel, white-faced, raised a hand suddenly. "Listen!" she said. From far below them, perhaps from that resounding chamber of the bats, there came an echo, flinging back and forth. It was the echo of a laugh. "Pinprickel!" cried Dulcibel, and then she sobbed.

They climbed back toward the surface. There was nothing else to do. By the boulders at least they would have fresh air and sunshine and some kind of shelter at night. James felt very much to blame. They should have stayed quietly in the inn, waiting for Mildred. How right Dulcibel had been when she had cried, "Something awful is going to happen." Something awful had happened—something too awful to contemplate. Then he remembered Mildred's warning him and saying that pleasant as it was to visit "these people" that "one must never become too involved in their lives," that "it always led to trouble" as indeed it had. But, he reminded himself, Dulcibel had come to him for help, and he had tried to help her. All these thoughts went through James's mind as wearily they made their way up toward what he thought of as "the surface." And what might await them there?

A bright summer morning awaited them. They could see the deep blue of the sky from the bottom of the shaft below the boulders. With a strange courage, born of their despair, they both felt a longing to get out. Out—even for a few minutes. *Out!* They climbed the boulders again, passed through their last night's sleeping place, in and out of strange spaces among the rocks, until once more they were on the smooth surface of the topmost boulder. There again was the almost familiar view, but more beautiful this time: the sun, rising higher, lit many little rivulets that wound their silvery way across the soggy, bright green pasture. They had been born of the storm.

"It's rather like Ireland," said James, who had once spent a holiday there, "the castle and all. . . ." Again, for some reason, he spoke in a whisper. There were no cattle and very little sound: only a watery murmur from somewhere quite close.

"Let's go down and find the spring," whispered James. "I'm thirsty. Aren't you?"

"I'm hungry," said Dulcibel. "And I'm frightened." She was staring unhappily at the smoke.

James glanced across at the castle. "It's all right: there are no windows or anything on this side. And even if he did see us, we'd be down the crevice before he could get to us. Come on."

They climbed down without speaking, intent on balance and sudden spaces between the stones. The ground below was still spongy from the rain, but the grass gleamed with a jewel-like brilliance. The hollow sound of trickling water became louder. "It must be round to the front," whispered James: by "the front" he meant the side of the rocks that faced the pasture and the castle. He did not know why he whispered: perhaps because this was unknown territory and he was following the instincts of a tracker.

Dulcibel, just as quietly, followed him around the curve of the rock. Yes, there lay the pool, overhung slightly in a cave-like way by the great boulder above. From the hollow sound of the trickling water, he guessed that the spring itself was somewhere within this shallow cavern. It was a very beautiful pool, edged with sweet-smelling plants—like water forget-me-not, spearmint, and maiden-hair. Very full now, after last night's storm, it reflected the sky. Dulcibel, ignoring the wet grass, sank down beside it on her heels, her skirts spread wide.

Suddenly James, about to kneel and drink, was aware of another odor—not so sweet. Where did it come from? A dead sheep perhaps? And then he saw a curious object across the pool from where he stood but close beside the rock. A great stone, it looked like, overhanging the water, covered by long and grayish dead grass. As he gazed, it moved slightly, and he saw, with a shock almost of disbelief, that that hair-like grass *was* hair—actual hair on a huge, great head. It was hair on the head of the giant.

Stooping, one finger to his lips, he touched Dulcibel's shoulder and pointed across the pool. She stared uncomprehendingly, and then her eyes widened and she gave a great start as though about to spring to her feet. He pressed on her shoulder to hold her still. If they valued their lives, they must not, for the moment, move or speak. Then, thought James, their only hope was to slink silently among the stones.

The giant, staring so intently into the depths of the pool, must be lying stretched out on the ground in front of the pile of boulders. As they watched, they saw a great hand come out and hover over the water. It was a filthy hand with broken, cruel nails. He held it poised for a second or two and then gently began to lower it. It slid beneath the surface with infinite stealth. The water hardly rippled. Suddenly, with a sharp plop, something leaped out of the pool and fell into Dulcibel's lap. She shrieked. But before the giant could look up, James had seen what it was and, with a lightning snatch, had grabbed it from her skirt and pushed it into the pocket of his jacket. He had seen the gleam of jade and the sparkle of the jewel.

The giant, amazed, was staring at them across the pool. He had a terrible face—inhuman and pitiless—and, like his hand, it was filthy. He began to smile, a very knowing, evil smile, showing his blackened teeth, and shoving himself backwards from the edge of the pool, rose slowly to his feet.

He towered above the pile of boulders, which hid his body from the waist down. He was clothed (if clothed it could be called) in a ragged patchwork of decaying skins. These—or perhaps it was the giant himself—smelled very unpleasant. He looked from one child to the other: which of them, his cunning gaze seemed to ask, had snatched his frog?

The two children stared back at him, unable to move or to speak. They were poised to run, but in what direction? White-faced, they watched as the giant, clumsy in his haste, lumbered around the rocks to the far edge of the pool. It lay between him and them, but with those great legs, one stride might take him across it. They could see the whole of him now, and none of it was pleasant. He seemed to be gauging the distance across the pool, one great hand on the boulder in order to steady himself, but as he lunged forward, his foot slipped on the soft mud and the whole weight of his body was thrown against the boulder. It was the same boulder on which, so few minutes before, they had sat so peacefully. They saw it teeter, then begin to tip. The giant, now floundering in the pool, saw it too, and for one swift moment, it distracted his attention.

Dulcibel ran then. Panic-stricken and sobbing, she ran in the direction the cattle had taken. James shouted after her, "Not that way, Dulcibel!" Other rocks were shifting and falling. There was a crashing, a rolling, and a settling. No hope now of escape by the crevice. James flew around the pool, where the giant was still floundering, and ran toward the edge of the Bluff—or where, as it was some way distant, he thought the edge would be. Dulcibel had heard his shout, it seemed, for she turned in an arc, making in his

direction. The giant, out of the pool now (to him, it was little more than a puddle) came lumbering after. There seemed no hurry in his strides, but at each step he covered a vast stretch of ground. He was going to cut Dulcibel off. Her curving run and change of direction had put her straight in his path. James, still well ahead, came within shouting distance of Dulcibel. "It's all right!" he kept yelling. "He can't hurt us. We've got the frog!"

"You have!" she screamed back, running faster than ever.

Suddenly, from behind them, came a great roar, as though of pain and anger. There was a crashing sound, and the ground beneath them shook. The giant must have tripped and fallen. They tried to run even faster. He would be up and after them, of that they felt sure, but it gave them a few minutes' grace. Except for such a chance as this, those colossal strides would quickly overtake them. There seemed nowhere to run to except along the top of the Bluff. This, James thought, was their safest course: the overhanging cliff would support the weight of two light children but not the thundering bulk of a running giant. And the giant would know this, unless in his blind hate and fury he might take the risk and they would all go crashing down together.

"Steady now, steady!" called out a voice suddenly. It was a familiar voice. James turned and, in turning, he saw the giant still lay where he had fallen, and then—sitting on a rock close by—he saw a stocky figure, smoking a pipe. It was Jack-of-the-Beanstalk.

James stood stock-still in amazement, and Dulcibel, after a swift look behind her at the prostrate giant, came up beside him. Lovingly, happily, they approached the old man. His ruddy face was even more glowing than usual: he exuded contentment and some secret kind of pride. "What would ye be doing up here?" he asked them. "Jack and I have been out and about—most of the night, I reckon. We thought ye were asleep in your beds. Have ye got wings or something?"

They told him their story. He listened and nodded and drew on his pipe. He did not seem surprised at anything they told him: in fact, at the end of their recital, they felt that the thrilling tale of their adventures had fallen rather flat. Except for one or two nervous glances from the children, no one referred to the prostrate giant. From this distance, dressed in his filthy patchwork of half-cured skins, the fallen giant seemed part of the landscape—a rotting tree trunk, perhaps, or an outcrop of mildewed rock.

"But how did *you* get up here?" asked James, at last.

The old man took his pipe out of his mouth. His smiling glance turned from one to the other, wreathed with delight and mystery. "Come you here, and I'll show ye."

He led them to the edge of the Bluff, toward a succulent, leafy bush unlike any they had seen before. The head of this bush had been bent so that it touched the ground and was pinned into it by what looked like a pair of antlers. Beside the antlers lay the heavy stone with which he had driven them in. "Take tight hold of the stem, and look ye down," he said.

They looked down. There, below them, was the village, and the streets were full of people. A colorful crowd, whose faces were too distant to be distinguishable, but they could see the waving of hands and kerchiefs as Jack appeared on the edge of the Bluff and could hear murmur of voices and the faint strains of a band. James wondered if Mildred was among them.

"Well," said Jack, "what about *that* for a beanstalk?"

Then James saw that the bush was not a bush at all, but the head of a vast plant writhing below them up the face of the cliff; because of the distance, at the foot it seemed to dwindle to nothing. "Came up in one night, like the other one," old Jack told them proudly. "Come away from the edge and I'll tell ye."

They sat beside him on the rock, and when he had filled his pipe, he said, "Came to me in the night—the night before last it was. I was sitting there by the fire, after you'd gone to bed, and I was thinking of that muck. You know that pile of muck at the foot of the Bluff, thrown down by the giant? Good, rich stuff, I thought to myself, and well matured. Couldn't get it out of my mind, like. Then up I gets and opens the case on the wall. I takes out the bean and I looks at it. A good, healthy bean, I thinks to myself. Always kept it well oiled—for the look of it, you know—so it weren't shriveled up and that. Now, I thought to myself, say I soak this bean in a barrel of warm water for an hour or two, to soften the skin like, and make a nick in it with a very sharp knife, there's no knowing what might happen. So that's what I did, and took it down the village and planted it into the muck. Then I came back to bed and slept like a baby. Now, there was all this rain in the night, you remember?" Dulcibel and James did indeed remember.

"This morning early, I thought I'd go round and take a look. Wasn't expecting anything much, mind you. Too many false hopes like in the past. And that's what I found!" He jerked his head toward the bunched greenery at the cliff edge. "Waved about in the wind a bit on the way up, but I've anchored her down like now, good and proper. I'll let her pod and store the beans. Might have a whole crop of 'em next year. . . ." He was silent a moment, happily drawing on his pipe. Then he said, "Old Jack, of course, was up in a trice—always wanted to have a go at that giant. Here he comes now, pleased as punch."

The children turned and saw the other Jack approaching. In one hand he carried his sling, which he swung about in a careless, happy way; in the other, a bunch of dirty, grass-like hair. "Got him in one," he called as he came within earshot.

"But where were you?" asked James.

"Large as life beside a thorn bush." He jerked his head toward Dulcibel. "He was after her and she ran right past me. But I steadied my hand and got him in one. Dead as a doornail. Just in time, I reckon, or he'd have done her a bit of mischief, I wouldn't wonder." He looked down at his sling and swung it proudly.

"Good as new," he remarked, "if not better." He looked up again, suddenly puzzled. "But how did ye come to be on the Bluff in the first place?"

They told their story again, and suddenly, feeling a movement in his pocket, James remembered the frog. How could he have forgotten it? He drew it out very gently, holding it in the palm of one hand and stroking it softly with the other. It was a lovely little creature, pale jade in color with a skin that felt like silk. In the crown of its head, set in something that sparkled, gleamed a jewel the color of an emerald. It half-closed its amber eyes in a contented sort of way, and something pulsated in its throat.

The old men leaned forward, expressing surprise and admiration. "Say he kept it by some water at the castle, some well or spring or some such, what with everything overflowing . . . all those rivulets and what not . . . it must have got swept away."

"And he'd know where to look for it all right," said Jack-of-the-Beanstalk.

"And he'd found it," said James. "That's what he was staring at. That's why he didn't see us—"

"Jumped right into her lap, you say! You'd never credit it!" And they examined the frog again, delighted with its beauty.

James held out his hands to Dulcibel. "You take it, Dulcibel—it's yours."

Dulcibel felt about her frieze skirt. "I haven't anywhere to put it," she said. James felt in the other pocket of his jacket and drew out the crumpled linen bag in which Mistress Tab (so long ago, it seemed now) had packed their luncheon. Very gently, they slid the frog inside and drew up the drawstrings tight, and then James knotted them. "She can breathe through this stuff," he said. James tied the bag onto Dulcibel's bodice by the ribbons threaded through the eyelet holes. "Now nothing can ever harm you," he said. She looked back at him. It was a wonderful moment: there seemed no need for words.

THIRTEEN

Climbing down was comparatively easy. Jack-of-the-Beanstalk went first to show them how to do it ("Keep in close to the stem and don't look down"). Dulcibel went next with her frog, and then James, who found that "don't look down" rule not really necessary: the leaves were so dense and wide that, glancing below for footholds, one could see only greenery. The ground came as a surprise, and so did the cheers of the crowd as he made his way down the mound of squelchy muck. People were shaking hands with Jack-of-the-Beanstalk and patting him on the back. He looked very happy. Another great cheer went up for Jack-the-Giant-Killer when he appeared, holding aloft the tress of giant's hair. He brandished it about his head, as he walked among the crowd, to murmurs of admiration and amazement. There were questions about the children, but all the looks were friendly as the people followed them across the Green toward the door of the inn. Many wanted to come inside and celebrate, but Jack-the-Giant-Killer, raising his hand again, pleaded courteously for quiet. They were weary, he said, and needed sleep. Later on he would speak to them and tell them the whole story, and there would be more to tell, he assured them, "than they would ever credit."

The old men, the two heroes of the hour, had meant what they said and took to their beds. Dulcibel and James went to the settle by the fire. It had its back to the window, through which several of the villagers were curiously peering. Here, the children felt more

private and could show Dame Wellbeloved the magic frog while she, in her turn, brought out the golden dress, which now shone and twinkled with its old luster. She had also "rubbed up" the little circlet of pearls. After she had left them, taking with her Dulcibel's scuffed and muddy golden slippers to see what she "could do with them," James turned to Dulcibel and said, "Dulcibel, I must talk to you."

Dulcibel, caressing the frog, inclined her head. "Look, she likes me already. What should I feed her on?"

"You must try different things," said James. "But listen, Dulcibel—"

"Perhaps," said Dulcibel, "she lives on air and pure spring water. . . ."

"Most likely," said James, "but, Dulcibel, I've been thinking things over, and there's something I've got to say to you—"

"Yes?" said Dulcibel, still dreamily stroking the frog.

"It's this," said James, "and it's serious. When you get back to the palace, before you do anything else, you must go straight to the well and agree to marry the toad."

"What!" cried Dulcibel. She turned and stared at him, amazed, nearly dropping the frog.

"Put that frog back in that bag," said James sternly.

Dulcibel, her face very pale, slowly did as she was told. "Agree to marry the toad!" she repeated. What new horror, her expression seemed to say, was about to come upon her? "You must be mad. . . ." she said falteringly.

"Not at all," said James. "I've thought the whole thing out. It's like this: as long as you've got that frog, nothing can hurt you. Right?"

"I suppose so," said Dulcibel.

"So long as you've *got* it—that's the point," went on James. "That frog has changed hands several times. Other people may have their eye on it. Now do you see what I mean? Why, you nearly dropped it a moment ago. Suppose we'd been sitting out of doors, in long grass, say?"

"But we weren't," said Dulcibel faintly.

"Where do you intend to keep it? When you get home, I mean."

Dulcibel was ready for this one. "In a little crystal pool, edged with precious stones, surrounded by a fence of wrought gold in filigree."

"Much good that'll be," said James. "No, Dulcibel, *while* you've got this frog in your possession, while you *know* you've got it, you must go straight to the well and promise to marry the toad. Suppose you lost the frog—and it could happen—where would you be? You'd have the same old worry hanging over you again for ever after. You must do it now, while you're safe. While you know for certain nothing can harm you."

Dulcibel was silent. Thoughtfully, she was tying the draw-strings of the bag to the ribbons of her bodice. "I'll think about it," she said, at last.

"It's the only way," said James. He wandered to the window. The peering faces had gone, but he could hear voices at the back door. Dame Wellbeloved, cleaning Dulcibel's slippers, was no doubt telling her story. By now most of the village would know that there was a princess at the inn, and which princess, and why. He sat down on the window seat and stared out at the Green. He had troubles of his own. Where was Mildred? Suppose she never came back: would he have to live in this strange country forever? He thought of his mother, of his own room, of his chemistry set and experiments just begun; he thought of the new bicycle he had been promised for his birthday. . . .

After a while, the two old men came down refreshed. Unselfishly, their first concern seemed to be with getting Dulcibel safely back to the palace. The miller's white horse was brought out and scrupulously groomed. Mane and tail were washed, braided, and decked with ribbons. The blacksmith unearthed an antiquated sidesaddle, made partly of wood and partly of leather. Willing hands scrubbed and polished, and, at the last, the gilder came with his pot of gold and put in the finishing touches. A piece of tapestry was produced, brilliant but slightly moth-eaten. Luckily, the vast sidesaddle hid the moth holes, and the effect was very fine. The horse enjoyed these ministrations: no one, not even his friend the miller's son, had paid him so much attention.

The day was still young: all had been up so early. At the inn, the meal they all partook of was nearer to breakfast than to luncheon. After this, Dulcibel's hair was washed and combed into a silky cloud. Dame Wellbeloved fussed about her as she changed into her usual finery. Even James, when he saw her, thought that she looked "quite nice." Dulcibel herself seemed excited and happy. The miller's son was to lead the horse, and most of the villagers decided to follow as far as the gates of the palace. The old men could not go as far as that: one Jack had to prune off the top growth of his beanstalk, the other to wash and dress the giant's tress. James could not go that far because Mildred might arrive.

The linen bag was discarded for one of plum-colored velvet, heavily embroidered with gold. It was lined with scarlet silk, and a golden tassel hung at each bottom corner.

"It could breathe better in the linen one," said James. "This one's too long and too deep."

"But it's open at the top," said Dulcibel, showing him. Lovingly, she placed the frog in the depths of the bag, peered in at it, then fastened the two top edges together with a golden pin. "There!" she said, smiling.

"Where did you get that pin?" asked James.

"Dame Wellbeloved. But I'll give it back to her again."

While they waited for the horse to be brought around (the gilt was not yet quite dry on the saddle), Dulcibel said to James, "I have to say it in rhyme."

"Say what?" said James.

"This thing I've got to say to the toad."

James jumped up and came toward her. So excited he felt, that he laid his hands on her golden sleeves as primly she sat in her chair. "So you're going to say it, Dulcibel! Oh, Dulcibel, how marvelous!"

"Yes," said Dulcibel, "I've thought it over."

"I'll make you a rhyme," said James. "I'll make you a rhyme in a minute. . . ."

He rushed about, looking for pens, ink, and paper. The old men produced these at last, but the pen was a quill, which spluttered. As James scribbled fast, frowning and crossing out, Jack-the-Giant-Killer said to Dulcibel, "He's right, you know. You've got the frog, but you mustn't push your luck. Look Fate in the face and strike while the iron's hot."

"I'm not afraid," said Dulcibel.

They were silent for a while as James scratched on with the quill. At last he laid it down and, frowning heavily, stared at the paper. "I think this last one's the best," he said.

"Read it," said Dulcibel.

James cleared his throat:

> "No evil Fate can me betide
> With this fair talisman by my side
> So gladly will I be thy bride."

"It's very nice," said Dulcibel, after a moment. "What does 'betide' mean?"

"Something that sweeps over you, happens to you. . . ."

"I see," said Dulcibel. "Yes, I think it's lovely."

"Can you learn it by heart?"

"I'll try," said Dulcibel. "I'll learn it on the way," she added. "Give me the piece of paper, just in case."

FOURTEEN

It was a great send-off. James and the two Jacks followed the little procession as far as the clearing in the forest, where the miller's son—always more mindful of animals than of humans—watered the horse at the stream. Dulcibel did not dismount. She sat there quietly, the reins sliding loosely through her fingers, while the horse drank its fill. Her gaze was turned toward the path that would lead them to the palace. James wondered what she was thinking. The embroidered bag, hitched by a golden cord to the pommel of the saddle, made a vivid splash of color against the horse's neck. The older villagers, a little tired by now, grouped themselves about on the grass. Others, including the two Jacks, sat down on the fallen tree. Some of the children played tag.

It seemed strange, to James, to see this clearing so full of life and color: the clearing where Mildred had rested on that first day; where so hopefully he had searched for a toad and had built his waterfalls; where Dulcibel, distraught and sobbing, had told him her awful news and where, later, they had sat—befogged and helpless—eating gingerbread and cherries. She had come to him for help and he had helped her. He had helped her very much, but something, somewhere, was missing.

At last, the miller's son led the horse back up the slope. It was time to say good-bye.

The two Jacks moved forward. Dulcibel, on her great white charger, seemed very high and far away (in all senses of these words, James realized suddenly). If the old men had been able to reach her face, James thought they would have kissed it—to them, in spite of all her grandeur, she was still their "little maid." Instead, they kissed her downstretched hand. James, coming forward shyly, could not bring himself to do this. He just said, "Good-bye, Dulcibel": there were so many people about.

"Good-bye, James," said Dulcibel, looking down at him gravely. She parted her lips as though to say something more, but then she seemed to change her mind. James, staring up at her, said rather huskily, "Try to remember the rhyme."

"I know it already," said Dulcibel. For another brief moment they looked at each other without speaking; then Dulcibel gave a little kick on the tapestried flank of her great white horse and, with the miller's son at the bridle, began to move away.

James watched until the whole procession had disappeared among the trees, then, turning quickly, ran down to the edge of the stream. The old men, lighting their pipes, went back to sit on the tree. There was no great hurry now. The story for them had ended.

James stared at the stream for quite a while without really seeing it, and then, quite suddenly, he noticed: due to the storm, the waters had swollen. All his little piles of stones had been swept away; the dry, tough moss on the larger boulders was dry no longer. In a day or two, he guessed, it would be green once more. The forget-me-nots on the verge barely held their heads above water. Some had been trampled into the mud by the hooves of Dulcibel's horse. There was something fierce and muscular in the rhythmic flow of the water: the stream in a different mood. He heard a frog croak, very faint it sounded above the gallop of the water. A frog? He stared across at the farther rocks, and then he saw it, wet and gleaming in the pale sunlight, gleaming so brightly in its wetness that one hardly noticed the jewel in its head.

James stared incredulously. He saw the gently throbbing throat, the contented, half-closed eyes. Relaxed and happy, it sprawled on the soaking moss.

James had been still, but now, mindless with shock, he kicked off his moccasins and, clumsy with haste, stooped to roll up his trousers. When he raised his head, the frog was gone. He stood there helplessly, one trouser leg up, the other down, as the stream rushed past him in its undulating pattern. Anyway, it was too deep and too fierce to be forded with any safety.

He stood for what seemed a long time among the wet forget-me-nots. Had the pin worked loose with the movement of the horse? Or had there been room on either side of the pin for a stifled creature, scenting running water, somehow to slither out? Or—? But what was the use of guessing? The frog had gone, and there was nothing he could do.

He thought of it—free, at last, back in its natural world, where grasses were fresh and damp and rock pools dark and secret. He tried not to think of Dulcibel.

After a while, he picked up his moccasins, rolled down his trouser leg, and made his way slowly up the slope. As he approached the old men and saw how tranquil they seemed, so peacefully puffing their pipes in the sunshine, exchanging a word here, a remark there, he paused. How *could* he tell them? He imagined their sudden dismay, the swift change of expression from contentment to shocked anxiety, the unkind clouding of their dream. "Black fly!" Jack-of-the-Beanstalk was saying confidently. "There'll be no black fly, not if I can help it. . . ." And Jack-the-Giant-Killer, nodding sagely in agreement, knocked out his pipe on the tree. Looking up, he saw James and rose to his feet.

"Well," he said, stretching slightly, "we'd best be getting along. Wouldn't be surprised if we found Mildred there by now."

On the way home, the old men talked of their plans: how a few kegs of gunpowder at a safe distance from the village might bring down a part of the Bluff. "Lot of good hard core in that overhang," explained Jack-the-Giant-Killer. "Say we all put our hands to it, we'd build a causeway, curving it around like—to keep the slope mild. Lot of good land up there, and cattle galore. And if it's good beans you're after, you don't want to go tearing up and down that beanstalk. Fair wear it out after a while. . . ."

"I got to go up for the pinching out," explained Jack-of-the-Beanstalk.

"Up!" exclaimed Jack-the-Giant-Killer. "Say we had the causeway, you could start at the top and go *down*."

On another occasion, James would have liked this talk, but on this one he barely listened. He lagged behind a little, hands in the pockets of his jacket, and head down-bent in thought.

Close beside the inn, a man was unharnessing a horse from a small cart. It was Little Hans. Then Mildred must be back? But it was not so. Little Hans explained to them that the last he had seen of Mildred was when he had put her down at the gates of the palace. She had produced her pass and was admitted immediately. He himself had mingled with the crowds of people and vehicles scattered about the outer park. In fact, none of the passengers he had taken to the wedding had come back with him: he had picked up quite a different load. The crush and muddle, he explained to them, had been worse this time than any other he remembered. "But she'll get a lift all right," he reassured them.

James went to his little room and wept. He wept for quite a long time, sitting on the edge of his truckle bed. Then, after a while, he dried his eyes and blew his nose on the little linen bag. Then he lay down on his back and ate a few apples and began to feel better. It was not long before, with one chewed apple in a listless hand, he fell asleep.

When he awoke, it was to the sound of Mildred's voice, a high-pitched twittering just outside his window. "Oh—thank you," she was saying, "thank you so very much. So very kind. I really can't thank you enough. . . ." It was dusk already. How long had he been asleep? He ran to the casement window and struggled with the latch. Then he remembered old Jack's dislike of hobgoblins and ran, instead, down the passage to the main room. Both Jacks were already at the front door, and there was Mildred on the threshold, a little breathless and clutching a bulging satchel. "Good night, and thank you again," she called out over her shoulder. There was no reply, and James, peering into the dimness, saw a white horse being led away into the shadows. He recognized it at once, even in the half-light: it was the miller's horse, the one that had carried Dulcibel, and beside it walked the miller's silent son. "He never spoke a word to me the whole way back," said Mildred with a laugh. "How good to see you all," she went on, coming into the lamplight, "and what a time I've had!"

"Where have you been?" asked James, rather grumpily, as Jack-the-Giant-Killer placed a chair for her beside the fire. She sat down thankfully.

"Everywhere. Just everywhere—or so it seems to me. First this wedding. Very well done. So many old friends. The notes I took. Just look at this satchel! I'll never sort them out. What wouldn't I have given to have had a camera . . . but never mind." She turned to Jack-of-the-Beanstalk. "You were quite right about the roads and the people. A few rough elements. Some damage in the park. But, once inside the palace, it was quite delightful. And the bride's dress . . . but I won't go into that now. There's something even more exciting which I can't wait to tell you. You see, I stayed on for an extra day or two—to keep them company, you know; there's always a bit of a sadness after a wedding—and while I was there news came of some terrible calamity which had befallen poor Boofy and Beau. I said to the dear Queen—the bride's mother, you know—'I must go to them, in case, just in case, there might be something I can do.' They were so understanding, so very kind, and put a coach at my disposal. I knew, James, you'd be all right here with our two dear Jacks—as I see you have been, thanks to their kindness. When I got to the palace, I can't describe the turmoil: the ball had fallen into the well, the golden ball, you remember? There had been darkness, and thunder and lightning, bad fairies laughing in the shadows, the whole thing! But to crown it all, Dulcibel had disappeared. No one knew where she was. Boofy was prostrate in her room, couldn't see anybody but, dear thing, sent down word I was to be looked after. They put me in the Blue Room, which I always find rather drafty. Beau, as you know, is never very talkative at the best of times. I couldn't get a word out of him. Almost as bad as that boy who brought me here." She laughed. "But, anyway, I did my silly best to cheer things up a little, describing the wedding and who was there and all the little bits of gossip. But it wasn't any good. They were all convinced that they were going to disappear into thin air, palace and all—*unless* they could find Dulcibel. But Dulcibel had vanished. Very odd, the palace being so closely guarded . . ." At this point, James nearly mentioned the key of the postern gate, but thought better of it: it had slipped her memory perhaps, and a reminder might upset her. "Well," went on Mildred, drawing a long breath, "the most extraordinary thing happened. I was awakened this morning —we'd all gone to bed very late the night before—by the sound of voices at the gates. I ran out onto the terrace. We all did, except Boofy. And there, on a snow-white charger, richly appareled, *was* Dulcibel, surrounded by what seemed to be a crowd of village people. Pumpkin flew in to fetch Boofy. We all hung over the terrace (there were several other royalties there—relations, you know) as the halberdiers threw open the gates and Dulcibel rode in. Then the halberdiers closed the gates again against the crowd. She rode in alone, her head held very high, and—it was the oddest thing—she did not even glance up at the terrace. She rode straight up two flights of marble steps, through the lemon trees up to the well, where she reined in her horse. We were all very quiet, holding our breaths: it was all so strange, you see. And then she said, in a loud clear voice:

> " 'Whatever ill may me betide
> I will gladly be thy bride.' "

James groaned. He put his hands to his brow and rocked slowly from side to side.

"What's the matter, James?" asked Mildred sharply. "You're not ill, are you?"

James raised a drawn face. "She didn't say *that*, did she?"

"Yes," said Mildred, "or something like it—"

"Oh, goodness!" exclaimed James, in a voice of utter despair.

Mildred looked at him in a very puzzled kind of way. "But it worked," she said. "No sooner had she spoken, than a young man sprang up on the curb of the well. Dressed, well I can't describe how he was dressed, deep green, slashed with scarlet, a wonderful cloak lined with—well, I couldn't quite see from the terrace. And, James, he had a crown on his head: he was a prince! And such a sweet, boyish face. A lovely smile. I spoke to him afterwards, just for a minute—to congratulate him, you know—and he was so very natural and unaffected. I shall always remember what he said to me—"

"What *did* he say?" asked James.

"He said 'Thank you very much.' His name is Florizel."

"It would be," muttered James.

"What did you say, James? I didn't quite hear—"

"I said—well, I mean—what a ghastly name."

Mildred looked hurt. "I think it's a beautiful name. And then of course we all slipped away into our rooms and got dressed. We had to. Poor Belle was in hair curlers—you know that fringe of hers? I did not stay for the party. I heard that the white horse was being taken off to Much-Belungun. Such a coincidence! I felt, perhaps, I ought to slip away. I just asked Boofy if she thought I might be allowed to address one little word to Prince Florizel, to wish them happiness, you know. And she took me up and introduced me–" Mildred paused as though an odd idea had struck her. "And yet, when you come to think of it, she had never met him before herself. Nothing for me, dear Jack!" she exclaimed as the old man came toward her with a bowl of soup. "I've been feasting for days, remember. All I want now is my little white bed"– she felt about for her gloves and satchel–"and it's so long since I've been in the saddle! I'll tell you the rest in the morning. . . ." She stood up, smiling down at James. "I hope he's been good," she said, turning to the old men. "I am so very grateful to you both. With all that's been going on, it has been such a comfort at times to think of you three here, in this quiet little house, where all is peace, all simplicity, and one quiet day's so like another. . . ."

Jack-of-the-Beanstalk took up a candle to light her up the stairs. She paused at the foot to say good night. "And sleep well," she said. "I know I shall." As she turned away, she gave a sigh: it was a very tired sigh, but, somehow, it sounded a happy one.

But James, in his bed, lay thinking for quite a while. He was thinking very hard about Dulcibel. Dulcibel had not needed a talisman; all she had needed was courage. And then he thought about Mildred and about all they would have to tell her in the morning. And of how and when they would get home again.

Home? He sat up in bed. There had been a loud noise. It was a familiar noise: the sharp bang of a car door. A car, a motor car? Yes, he could hear the engine running. And, from somewhere far away, he could hear the murmur of traffic. He jumped out of bed and ran to the window. It wasn't the casement: it was his own window. He drew aside the curtains. Yes, there was Smith Street, with its streetlamps. It was raining slightly. A taxi drew away from the house opposite, its taillight gleaming. A voice said, "See you on Tuesday." A front door closed loudly, and then the street was quiet again. He put on his bedside light. Yes, there was his picture of the running horse. Running, just as usual, not standing still and staring back at him. He went to the bathroom and, coming out, leaned over the banisters. There were lights downstairs—his parents were still up. He could hear their voices in the sitting room. The hall was the same old hall, with its two stuffed owls. There wasn't a shooting stick in the stand by the front door: they had never had a shooting stick. He went back to bed: the bedclothes were still warm. He put out the light and drew the eiderdown up around his ears. Very soon he was asleep again and dreaming a long, lovely dream about cosmonauts.